Murder in Galena

A Karen Prince Mystery

by

Sandra Principe

ISBN: 0-9767954-1-8 (Paperback)

This book is printed on acid free paper.

Galena Pubishing – rev. 09/13/04

Acknowledgements

I would like to thank my family and friends who read the early version of this book for their time and comments, including Lina Haycraft, Laurie Principe, Counselors Therese Martin, Linda Puvogel, Jane McCullough, Carol Seelig, and James Drummond, Author Margo Drummond, and my Galena neighbors Lisa Melnick, Barbara Alexander, Judith Wehrle, and Sara Jean Gray. I also thank Susan Farber for the kind loan of her Waterford vase for the painting, "Butterfly Bouquet" which appears on the cover of this book, and Daryl Watson, Director of the Galena Historical Society, for sharing his knowledge of Galena's history with me.

Disclaimer

Dedication

To my family, with love and gratitude for your support.

Chapter
1

The Call

More improbable things have happened, but not many. Three months ago I was given an incredible gift: financial freedom, in the form of a winning lottery ticket. I didn't play the lottery regularly. I have no favorite numbers, at least I didn't before I won the $325,000,000 power ball game. Well actually, I won half. There were two winning tickets, mine and one bought by an office pool in Springfield, Illinois.

My name is Karen Prince. I'm forty-five years old, an artist, a painter actually, and lecturer on the subject of Dutch Floral paintings from 1600 to 1720. I live in a beautiful and little known corner of Illinois, along the Mississippi River. Most people think of rural Illinois as flat cornfields. But our little county was spared from the great leveling effect of the glaciers, which moved across the rest of the state. As a result, we still have our rolling tree covered hills and limestone bluffs. In fact, the area looks very much like the picture postcards of Maine and Vermont with trees glowing orange and red. It's October tenth, and we are in the peak of the color season. Oak and maple trees are glowing with fall color. I live with my Norwegian Forest cat, Truffles, in an old two story farm house, with an attached silo. The silo was an addition by a former owner who collected and renovated these fast disappearing old structures. The silo now contains a spiral staircase leading up to a viewing tower and my favorite spot, my studio.

This morning I was having my mandatory cup of coffee and working on plans for "Turning Points," the foundation I'm setting up with some of my lottery winnings, when my best friend, Alice, called. I picked up the receiver expecting a cheery hello, but heard only panic as she said, "I just found George!"

"Alice, is that you? What do you mean? You just found George?" George is Alice's "ex". They hadn't seen each other, to my knowledge, for over a year now. I couldn't make any sense out of what she said.

Alice sobbed into the phone. I could barely make out what she was saying, "He's lying by the pond—he's—he's dead!"

"What? Alice, are you all right? Are you alone?" I could feel my heart race, my senses kick into high alert.

"Yes—I'm here alone—I think—"

"I'll be right over. Don't touch anything. Use your cell phone and call 911. Just sit down, and I'll be there in five minutes. Are you up at the house?" The adrenaline upped the sound level of my voice so that I was shouting into the phone.

"I'm down at the pond. I'll be here. Hurry!"

"I will," I said and hung up the phone. I grabbed my purse and jumped into the Boxster. As I flew down Blackjack Road to Pilot's Knob, thoughts rushed through my mind—images of Alice, George and me in summers gone by, hiking our trails, then watching the sunsets and sharing stories. Alice and I met ten years ago at the opening of Alice's new gallery in Chicago. We immediately became friends and, since then, we've become more like sisters—the only "family" we each have. We've shared all of life's ups and downs for the past ten years. We are who we each list when asked, "Who to contact in the event of any emergency." And this was definitely an emergency. I thought of various possibilities and it seemed to me that George must have had a heart attack. He'd always looked like a heart attack waiting to happen—beefy red face, apple shape, with about twenty-five extra pounds around his belly.

I took a left off Blackjack Road and drove up the steep windy road. Alice's home was perched on Pilot's Knob, one of the highest points overlooking the Mississippi River for two hundred miles. Her home had been built by a wealthy riverboat captain in the 1840's, when Galena was a boom town and boats hauled precious lead ore from the local mines down the Mississippi to the South. It's hard to imagine, but Galena was the Chicago of its time. And Alice's house has all the hand painted wood, carved stairways, and extravagant balconies that a mansion of that time commanded. Unfortunately, the house is said to be haunted by the captain's ghost. These ghost stories give me the creeps, but I force myself to forget about them as much as I can.

As I turned into Alice's vertical drive, I took the first branch road to the right, which leads to her pond. The pond is on the lower portion of Alice's seven hundred acre tract. The stable and barn are down there as well and the house is on a clearing up above. There is a limestone bluff behind the stable and barn and a natural spring runs from the foot of the bluff along the side of the buildings, into the pond about a hundred yards away.

I left the Boxster in the circular drive in front of the stable and ran the hundred yards down to Alice. She made a lonely silhouette. A tall, thin, six feet, with long straight espresso colored hair, she stood in her country uniform of blue jeans and jacket, hovering over something. The something was George's body. George lay face up on the soggy ground at the edge of the pond. I put my arm around Alice and we stood staring at George as the piercing sound of the ambulance siren filled the air.

Lights flashing, the red and white ambulance came up the drive, passed the Boxster and drove across the field towards us. They stopped about fifty feet from us at the edge of the field, avoiding the marshy land closer to the pond.

As the siren wound down I looked up at Alice and asked, "Al, what was George doing out here?"

She shook her head, "I don't know. I just came down here this morning to check on the water level, and—" her voice dissolved into tears.

As she wiped the tears from her face I saw the blood on her hand and jacket sleeve. I pulled a Kleenex from my pocket and wiped the spot on her sleeve.

"Alice! What is this?"

She looked down at the blood on the Kleenex and then at her hand and jacket sleeve. "I don't know. I must have gotten it on me when I found him!" She burst into tears again.

"It's ok," I said, giving her another hug.

Two forty-something year old men, part of our volunteer rescue squad, approached us carrying a stretcher. I recognized John Walsh, the owner of the local lumber yard, as one of them. I'd purchased masonite boards from him for my painting panels. I didn't know the other fellow. John dropped to his knees next to George and checked for a pulse. I expected him to start CPR but he didn't. Instead, he turned George's head to the side, revealing an ugly gash. John looked at the two of us and pulled his phone from his pocket.

He spoke loudly into the cell phone, "Sheriff Olson? John Walsh. I'm out at the old Captain Tyler place. I think you'd better come out here."

Chapter 2

The Police

The sheriff and the coroner found the four of us at the pond. Well, I guess it was five of us counting George. Sheriff Olson took one look at the gash on George's head and called his chief detective to the scene.

Detective Cavanaugh, a stocky, rumpled looking man in his fifties, arrived quickly in a gray pick-up truck. The three of them conferred, the sheriff, the coroner, and the detective that is, as Alice, the two ambulance guys and I waited. We watched the detective take photos and make an outline around George in the grass, just like in an Agatha Christie novel. Only I don't think Agatha's police used orange spray paint as Detective Cavanaugh did here. Finally, they loaded George onto the stretcher and into the ambulance. The procession of ambulance, sheriff, and coroner made its way across the field and down the driveway heading for the Jo Daviess County Hospital.

Detective Cavanaugh asked Alice and me to come up to the house with him so we could answer a few questions. We arranged ourselves around the long oak dining room table, Alice and I on one side, Cavanaugh on the other. I studied him for a minute and took in his long bristly moustache, round black eyes, and prominent pink nose. Cavanaugh was wearing his long gray overcoat and as he reached into his back pocket to pull out a small spiral notebook I saw that he was remarkably out of shape. He reminded me of one of the gray opossums that waddled across my deck at night.

Detective Cavanaugh cleared his throat and began his questions. We gave him our names, phone numbers and addresses. I told the detective about my call from Alice and that I hadn't seen or heard from George since their divorce.

Then Cavanaugh turned his attention to Alice and asked, "When was the last time you spoke with George?"

5

There was a pause before she said, "Last week." The answer surprised me and I looked at her quizzically.

"He called me looking for the papers for Challenger, one of his horses. He couldn't find them and thought maybe I had the file."

"Did you know he was coming here?" the detective asked.

"No, I had no idea. I told him I was sure I didn't have any of his papers. But he asked me to look in the stable when I got out here Friday night and I said I would."

Detective Cavanaugh undoubtedly knew Alice commuted from Chicago each weekend. Galena is a small community. The local residents knew each other and the rest of the homeowners are weekenders from Chicago.

"And did you do that, check for his papers?" Detective Cavanaugh asked.

"Yes, when I got out here Friday afternoon, I unpacked the car and went directly out to the stable. I looked through the file cabinets in the office where he thought they might be, but I didn't find them. He'd kept all the horses after the divorce and I know he took all their papers."

"And did you tell George you couldn't find the papers?"

"I tried to let him know, but I couldn't reach him. I left a message on his cell phone."

"Did you telephone his house?"

"No, I never call his house. I don't want to hear her voice."

"Whose voice?" Detective Cavanaugh asked quickly.

"Darlene's, his new wife," Alice said, the anger and hurt clear in her voice.

"How long ago was that?"

"How long ago that I called him or how long ago that he married her?"

Detective Cavanaugh cleared his throat then said, "That he married her."

"We've been divorced for twelve months now. George and Darlene were married the day our divorce was final." There was a silent moment before Alice continued, "George left me about a year before our divorce. That tramp was his personal trainer and a bad one at that. He never did lose any weight. Anyway, let's see, that makes it just about two years ago that they—started exercising together, shall we say."

"And what kind of contact have you had with your "ex" since the divorce?"

"Well, none at first. Then George started calling me about six months ago. First, he had questions about the Chicago house—the repair people, the furnace, that kind of thing."

"And besides the phone calls, have you met with him?" The detective picked his way through the questioning, trying to elicit information and side step the venom Alice spewed when discussing George and his fourth wife.

"I've met with George a few times."

"And has he been out here since your divorce?"

"No. Not that I know of anyway. This is my house and I'll be damned if he's going to set foot on my property with her."

"Did he ever come out here alone?" the detective asked again.

"Like I said, not that I know of, and certainly not with my permission! This is my life now and he is definitely not a part of it."

"I see," said the detective. "But he was here last night."

"Well, apparently. I didn't see him though and I didn't know he was here."

"Do you think he was here looking for those papers?"

"I have no idea. I suppose he could have been."

"And how would he have gotten here? Is his car here?" Detective Cavanaugh asked.

"I haven't seen his car and I have no idea how he got here," Alice said.

She was sounding defensive, and I didn't like it. The two of them stared at each other for a minute.

"Was anything out of place in the house when you arrived here last night?" he asked.

"What do you mean?" Alice said.

"I mean, did it look like anyone had been in your house while you were gone this week?"

"Well, the cleaning lady had been here. She lets herself in and out," Alice said.

"Anything to suggest someone else had been here?"

"No, I didn't notice anything unusual."

7

"What about this morning?"

"Nothing I noticed."

"Did you hear anything during the night?"

"No, I didn't. I went to bed early and woke up around six-thirty. I made coffee and went down to the pond. Oh, wait a minute. I did notice something was missing. But I figured the cleaning lady had put it somewhere, or taken it to be fixed or something."

"And what was that?" Cavanaugh asked, his eyes focusing more sharply on Alice.

"The fireplace iron," Alice said. "I went to make a fire in the kitchen and I noticed the fire iron was missing. I didn't think much of it at the time."

"The fire iron from the kitchen fireplace was missing you say?" Detective Cavanaugh repeated, making notes in his little book.

"That's right," Alice said.

"Thank you, Ms. Almonte. You've been very cooperative. I have to ask you not to leave the area. I may have more questions for you. I'd like to take some fingerprints before anyone else arrives. I'm going to post an officer at the gate. I don't want anyone else on the property for now. If you and your friend, Karen, could just wait in here."

I hadn't realized the detective had someone with him. He must have called him on his way over.

With that, Detective Cavanaugh pushed back his chair with a great squeak of wood against wood and moved his large frame into the adjoining kitchen. In a minute though, he was back, his great mustache pushed forward by his pursed lips.

"What is the meaning of the noose hanging from the rafters on the porch?"

"Oh, that was a joke. You know the original owner died in a ship wreck and his wife hung herself in this house. Their spirits are supposed to haunt the place. Someone gave us that noose as a sort of macabre house warming gift and, well, we hung it there as a joke. I should take it down really—" Alice said, her voice trailing off.

Chapter 3

The Boyfriend

Detective Cavanaugh busied himself sprinkling white powder over door knobs, table tops and window sills in the five rooms on the first floor.

"Can I make you some tea?" I asked, not quite sure what would comfort Alice right now.

She gave me a raised eyebrow look. I should have known better. "Well, it is early," I said, in my own defense. "I'll mix you a Bloody Mary then."

"Stiff, thank you," she said, nodding her head.

As I handed her a frosty glass of red tomato juice and vodka, there was a knock at the front door. The door's glass panel was large and revealed a small man in a brown sheriff's uniform standing next to a six foot four inch hulk. The larger fellow was Donald Strong, Alice's boyfriend. Donald, a Chicago real estate developer, is extraordinarily good looking, well groomed, and has the chiseled muscles only people who spend three hours a day in the gym can achieve. Alice looked startled at the sight of him.

"Donald! I'd forgotten he was coming out here. Oh, look at me—and the police—oh, no—" Alice murmured to me.

Detective Cavanaugh quickly came back into the living room and walking by us determinedly, opened the door. The small wiry officer announced in an unexpectedly low and loud voice, "This is Mr. Strong. Says he's here to see Alice Almonte."

Cavanaugh looked to Alice for confirmation. She was already on her feet saying, "Donald! Yes, let him in." Cavanaugh stepped aside and Donald came into the room and Alice's open arms.

Cavanaugh nodded to the officer and the fellow left, presumably to return to his post at the front gate. After giving Donald a hug and kiss, Alice turned to Detective Cavanaugh and made a more formal introduction. She briefly told Donald about finding George and explained that Detective Cavanaugh was just examining the house.

9

"I wonder if I could ask you a few questions, Donald?" Cavanaugh said.

"Sure. Fire away."

Cavanaugh retrieved his notebook and asked, "Did you know George Almonte?"

"No, never met him. I knew of him of course, as Alice's former husband."

"And where were you yesterday afternoon and evening?"

"I spent the afternoon in meetings, at my office. I left about six, went to the club and worked out, had dinner, and got home about ten. I was home until I left this morning to drive out here."

"Did you have dinner alone?"

"No, I had dinner with two real estate brokers I work with. We ate at my club."

"Their names?"

"Mary Donnelly and Jim Shaw."

"And the club?"

"Union League."

"One last question, what time did you say you left this morning?"

"I didn't say, but I left at seven this morning and drove straight here. One stop for gas. I have a receipt if you need it."

"No, no. Thank you. That should take care of it. I appreciate your cooperation Donald. I'm almost finished in here then I'll be going to the pond and the stable," Cavanaugh said. "I'll stop by the house again before I leave. My officer will still be at the lower gate. So, if you are expecting anyone else let me know. You're free to come and go. But please don't leave town without telling me how to get in touch with you."

"Of course," Alice said, answering for the three of us as she walked Cavanaugh to the door. "Would you mind letting me know the results of the autopsy when you have it?" Alice asked.

"Yes, it should be done by Monday afternoon. I'll call you then," the detective promised.

"I'll still be here. I don't think I'll go back to the city right away. I'll let you know as I make my plans," Alice said.

"Well, I'll be in touch." And with that the detective closed the front door behind him.

We moved into the kitchen and stood around the counter where I'd left the tomato juice and vodka. I poured myself a glass of water and offered Donald a drink. He waved off the vodka and had a glass of tomato juice as Alice recounted the morning's events in more detail.

"So, what do you think happened to George?" Donald finally asked Alice.

"I'd think it was a heart attack, but there's the bash on his head. And where's his car? And where is my fire iron?" Alice said.

"Maybe whoever he was with brought him here, hit him on the head, and left him. Or maybe they just brought him here after killing him, to throw the police off their trail. They could have stolen his car," Donald said.

The proffered alternatives all included one thing—murder. It wasn't looking like a heart attack any more.

"A lot of possibilities—," Alice said, her voice unusually weak. "Do you think it could have been an accident of some sort?" she asked.

"Well, if it was, why didn't whoever he was with call an ambulance instead of just leaving him?" I asked.

"Right. So it is—it looks like he was—killed," Donald said, looking from one of us to the other.

"It looks that way right now," I said, nodding.

"Who would have wanted to kill him?" Donald asked.

"Besides me, you mean," Alice said, sarcastically.

"Alice, don't even joke about that. Anyway, what would you have to gain? The divorce is over. If you were going to kill him, why wouldn't you have done it before the divorce?" I said.

"Oh, I didn't kill him, of course. But I certainly wished him dead more than once over the past two years," Alice said.

"Well, who else would have had a motive?" Donald asked.

"He was having terrible arguments with his son, Max," Alice said.

"I thought his son had moved out to California," I said.

"He did, but hey, that's what 'friends and family' phone rates are for. They kept in touch. Not exactly the picture in the commercials, but they talked, well, mostly fought, a lot. And just because he moved doesn't mean he couldn't have come back here," Alice said.

"True enough," I conceded. "And what about Darlene?" I asked.

11

"She would have a bundle to gain, I mean a r-e-a-l bundle," Alice said, stretching out the word "real" to convey that we were talking millions of dollars here.

"Unless there was some sort of prenuptial agreement," Donald said.

"I doubt there was," Alice said. "George was under some sort of spell when he married her. It was probably having sex again.   After the last five years of our marriage, I guess that was pretty exciting to him." Her sarcastic humor had the ring of truth to it.

"So, it could have been a robber, his wife, his son, anyone else in the group of likely suspects?" I asked.

"Don't forget me," Alice said.

"Besides you," I said, giving her a look.

"Maybe Rich, his old business partner," Alice thought out loud. "Rich will certainly be better off financially with George dead, but I don't really think he killed George because of that. I mean, he's wealthy in his own right. And they go way back. No, I don't think it would be Rich," Alice said, shaking her head.

"Well, someone killed him," I said. "And we're going to have to figure out who, so the police don't get any wrong ideas about you, my dear. You know, the person who finds the body is always a prime suspect in mystery novels," I said, looking at Alice.

"How about if we get out of here for a while and let the police do their job?" Donald said. "Can I take you two to lunch? You need to get some space between you and this horrific morning. And you do need to keep up your strength," he said.

I got the feeling that he wanted out of there himself. And I couldn't blame him. The creep level was reaching the ceiling.

"I should get home," I said. "I'll be there if you need me. You two go, get something to eat, and take your mind off of this for a while," I said, putting down my drink and gathering up my purse.

We moved toward the door and hugged our goodbyes.

"Call me later," I said and left the two of them to their lunch escape.

I drove down the gravel road, past the stable and barn, and the pond, to Pilot's Knob Road, stopping at the closed gate. The same officer who had escorted Donald to the house now opened the gate for me. A handful of neighbors stood peering into the property from the road. Listening to the police band radio is prime entertainment for some folks out here. A murder was big news and their trip to the scene would make for months of conversation.

Chapter
4

Misty Valley

Driving back home, my mind was racing as fast as the car's engine. Seeing George's body, talking to the police, it was all a shock. Although I loved reading murder mysteries, this was too real.

Still, as I took in each twist and turn of Blackjack Road I couldn't help but be overwhelmed by the stunning views—rolling hills, small farm fields edged with maple and oak trees glowing in autumn colors, a flock of wild turkeys pecking among the harvested rows of corn. I came to my property, marked by a stand of Eastern red cedar trees. The trees are covered with deep blue berries, a feast for the cedar wax wings flying in flocks of hundreds, from tree to tree, gathering fuel for their winter migration. I watch these migratory birds each fall as they swoop through. Yellowish gray, with a black mask across their eyes, they are a sort of berry bandit.

As I pulled up to my house, I saw Louise working in the rock garden along the drive. She was dressed in well worn jeans, knee high green garden boots, and a floppy straw hat. Louise and her husband Tony are a retired local couple, who have taken on the job of keeping my land in shape and watching the house and my cat, Truffles, when I travel. Louise is in the process of creating a new flower garden. This will be the tenth garden, a cutting garden, as all my gardens are, and a source of inspiration and models for my floral paintings. We designed this one to be in perfect viewing position from the screened in porch.

A chain saw buzzed in the woods. That would be Tony clearing some of this year's dead elms. Long gone from most cities, the tough old country elms still stood here, fighting their fight against the Dutch Elm disease that had taken their city cousins. Before moving here I thought of forest land as more or less static, seeing only the mature hundred year old trees. But it is a living organism, a changing succession of plants, animals and trees. Nothing stays the same. Just as people are always changing, growing, living—and dying.

I waved to Louise and went inside. Truffles greeted me with a trill and a purr, winding her furry body through my ankles as I made myself a cup of hot tea. The tea made and hellos said to Truffs, I sank into my favorite overstuffed lounge chair. Truffles curled into a warm black ball in my lap. I let my head sink back into the chair cushion, closed my eyes, and re-ran the events of the morning. I've read enough mystery novels to know that the person who finds the body is always a suspect. And Alice was the one who found George's body. To make matters worse, he was killed on her property, or at least his body was found there. And it is common knowledge that Alice was terribly hurt by George's divorcing her. It would be natural for the police to think of Alice as a prime suspect. Maybe whoever killed him intended to point the finger at Alice. There aren't many murders out here, and I wasn't willing to rely on the local police to vindicate my best friend, and the nearest thing to "family" I have left in this world. I decided to do my own investigation.

Our neighbor, Tonya, is having a party tonight and that'll be a good place to start. There should be some folks who've known George out here. I'll see what I can learn about George's business partner, and his son, and his new wife.

I finished my tea and checked the time—one-twenty. This gave me four hours before I had to get ready for tonight's event. I lifted Truffs from my lap and placed her on the chair where I had been sitting. With a bit of petting, she settled into the warmed cushions and I made my way up the winding stairs to my retreat—my studio.

When I enter my studio I feel like I'm entering a cathedral. Not that my studio is large or ornate. It's the quality of the light shining into the quiet darkened room from the tall north windows that gives me that feeling—that, and the reverence with which I paint. The heart and soul of my work is light, shining through darkness, revealing beauty. To create that atmosphere, I painted my studio walls a dark gray–green. This prevents light from bouncing around and allows me to actually see the light shining on the flowers I'm painting. The only windows are on the north wall. They start about five feet off the ground and are twelve feet high. This gives me that light streaming into darkness effect.

I paint for hours on end, so I usually sit to conserve my energy for the painting process. My oak easel is eight feet tall, with a crank arrangement that lets me raise and lower my canvas to the proper painting height. I have the easel to the right of the windows, so the light comes into the painting from the left. That is the way we are accustomed to seeing. We read from left to right and that is the way I place the light in my paintings.

My flower models were waiting for me in the fridge in my studio. I took them out and set them on the pedestal to the right of my easel and sat in my chair. Setting out the paints for the day is a ritual that lets the day's events fade from my mind. I spent the next four hours painting a cascade of pink Rugosa roses arranged in a glass vase. Painting often brings me into a time warp, where four hours goes by in what seems like a matter of minutes.

By five-thirty, I had several more roses on my canvas and the hard shinning surface of the vase was taking form. I pulled myself from this meditative world, flipped the overhead lights on in the studio, and cleaned my brushes and palette.

It was time to get ready for the evening's get together.

Chapter 5

The Party

Six-thirty is the standard time for our local parties. People out here tend to arrive on time and leave early. None of this fashionably late business for us country folk. It was six-forty when I pulled the Boxster into the mowed field in front of Tonya's. This makeshift parking lot was already filled with an assortment of country pick-up trucks and city cars. I spotted my favorite caterer's white van, the words "Elegant Eats" stenciled in large black letters on its side. Tonight's party was shaping up to be a culinary treat, as well a great place to do my research.

I let myself in the front door and said brief hellos as I made my way through the group of people gathered in front of the bar in the living room. As people got their drinks, they moved on to the kitchen and the new great room addition to Tonya's 1840 log cabin. A caterer circled the room offering shrimp, salmon and vegetables and guests caught up on each other's travel adventures. It was mostly Europe in the summer, Florida or Arizona in the winter. I favored the tropical allure of Hawaii in the winter and was quite content to stay here spring, summer and autumn. But, I didn't want to trade travel stories right now. I needed to find someone who could fill me in on George's life since the divorce.

I walked into the new great room looking for someone who could answer my questions and couldn't help but marvel at Tonya's decorations for this soiree. She spends weeks each year creating a visually interesting setting. This year, the tables featured collections of old photos, antique books, fall gourds and flowers. A four foot tall toy sheep dog had the center seat on the sofa. Sculptures and various prizes collected on Tonya's travels were set around the room. Large glass doors lead to the patio. Tonya had this spot lit to show the party extended outdoors as well. She had turned her patio into a faux pond, painting the cement baby blue, arranging decoy ducks floating on the patio, adding a path of stepping stones, and encircling the whole "pond" with large yellow mums. Beyond the patio, the flicker of flames and smoke rose from the fire pit. Guests could stroll out to the fire circle and get a breath of air throughout the evening.

Tonya herself was floating about the great room greeting guests in a pointy black witch's hat, complete with attached orange hair hanging down to her shoulders.

I spotted Ed Seller, who was standing alone, looking at the photos Tonya had arranged on the fireplace mantel. Ed was a Chicago doctor and had been coming out here for thirty years now.

"Hi, Karen," Ed said and kissed the air near my cheek.

"Hi," I said returning his air kiss. Strange custom this air kissing.

"What a shock to hear about George. It was a heart attack I assume?" Ed asked.

"Well, they're not sure about that, Doc," I said. "There may have been more to it than that. Alice wasn't expecting him out here. In fact, she didn't know he was here until she found him, lying there dead, this morning. George had been hit on the back of the head. They're doing an autopsy and won't be certain of the cause of death until Monday."

"How awfully sad for Alice. After all she's been through, then to find George like that," Ed said.

"I know. She's extremely upset, naturally. At least she has her friend Donald out here with her this weekend," I said.

Glancing up at the mantle next to us, I noticed there was a photo dated 1869, with a group of nine people standing in front of Tonya's home. I assumed these were the original inhabitants of this house. They looked into the camera with determined somber expressions on their gaunt dark faces. The sepia coloration added to the grim mood of the photo. The next picture was of a younger Tonya with a gentleman I had never seen.

"Was that Tonya's husband?" I asked Ed, picking up the photo.

"Yes, that was Will. He passed away just after they purchased this place, twenty-five years ago. He was just forty-five at the time."

"And who is this?" I asked replacing the photo of Tonya and picking up a silver framed eight by ten inch group photo. This photo was in color and depicted a gathering, much like tonight's. Looking at the people I knew in the photo, I guessed it was taken at least ten years ago.

18

"That's Tonya, me of course, George and Alice, Rich Fox—"

I interrupted, "Is that the fellow who was George's business partner?"

"Yes, he used to have a place out here as well."

"When was that, Ed?"

"Well, Rich bought out here, oh, I bet it was fifteen years ago, but he sold his place some six or seven years ago," Ed said. "Just before you moved out here I guess."

"What sort of business did Rich and George do together?" I asked.

"Well, as I understand it, they bought businesses out of bankruptcy for a penny on the dollar and then turned them around. They sort of got into that business by the backdoor. They went to law school together and when they graduated they set up their own law firm. They did all sorts of business law and started handling bankruptcies in the late 70's and early 80's when interest rates were eighteen percent and driving businesses under water. George told me their practice became more and more specialized in bankruptcy. They started seeing businesses that failed for reasons they figured they could cure, like internal fighting, or losing major clients due to mismanagement. They'd go in and buy these companies and turn them around. Did well, as I hear it."

"Did they get along with each other?"

"Hmmm, what are you thinking?"

"Just asking, that's all."

"They were best of friends for a long time, but they had a falling out a while ago. Rich stopped coming out here and then, as I say, he sold his place about seven years ago."

"Tell me about the businesses they owned," I said hoping Ed wouldn't feel I was asking too many questions. But Ed seemed to be enjoying recounting times gone by and he continued, "Well, they started out with a printing company. It'd been doing well while the fellow that started it was alive, but when his son-in-law took over he fired the long time employees who'd been making the company work and they lost their major customers. George figured he could get the customers back by rehiring the old employees and promising to meet delivery deadlines or refund the client's money. It was a gamble, but it worked."

"Do you know what George and Rich argued about?"

"Well, they had some differences of opinion about which businesses to buy, of course, but they respected each other and had a good relationship early on. Of course, it's easy to get along when you're making money hand over fist. The tougher times came with the 90's recession. Money tightened up and business came to a crawl for several years, especially in Chicago and California, where they were most heavily invested. George said they disagreed on the direction they should take and started dividing up their business. They still hold—I guess I should say held—a few companies in common. I haven't seen Rich for years now."

Marie, Ed's wife, came up and joined us. Marie is a pediatrician and practices at Northwestern Medical Center in Chicago. "What are you two gossiping about over here?" she asked, smiling as she joined us at the fireplace.

"Ed's filling me in on George's old partner, Rich."

"Oh, how awful about George," she said. "How is Alice taking all this?"

"It's shocking of course. She has her friend Donald out with her this weekend and I think that's some comfort for her."

"Heart attack I assume?" Marie asked.

"They're not sure. He has a gash on the head. The police don't know the cause of death yet."

"Really?" she said, her eyes widening. "We all assumed it was a heart attack, given his medical history."

"Maybe it was and he somehow hit his head when he fell. We don't know yet for sure."

"Oh, well, I hope for Alice's sake it was a heart attack. After all the divorce turmoil, the last thing she needs is a murder investigation!"

"I absolutely agree," I said.

Marie excused herself, no doubt to pass along the news of a possible murder. Ed offered to get me a drink, holding up his glass to indicate that he was on his way to refresh his own. I thanked him but declined. I wanted a clear head tonight. As Ed made his way to the bar, I decided to track down Polly and see what I could learn about George's latest wife and son. Polly had stayed friends with George, while most of the people at this party had dropped all connections with him after he divorced Alice.

Gliding through the crowd with a purposeful look, intended to dissuade the other guests from drawing me into conversation, I scouted the living room, dining room, and kitchen for Polly's blonde head. Not seeing her long hair and slim figure, I made my way out back to the bonfire. Only two other people were out there, one of whom was my target.

"Polly, hi," I said coming up next to her and warming my hands in the radiant heat of the fire. Ron, whose conversation with Polly I had clearly interrupted, gave me a somewhat forced smile and the standard hello punctuated with an air kiss.

"Hello, Ronny," I said, wondering what I had interrupted.

"I'm going to let you ladies talk. Can I get you anything, Polly? Karen?" Ron asked, looking from one to the other of us.

"Another champagne, please," said Polly, handing Ron her flute glass.

"I'm fine, thanks," I said. I was thinking I would have about five minutes alone with Polly if no one else interrupted us, as I had just interrupted Ron.

"So Polly, I assume you've heard the terrible news about George," I said, skipping preliminaries and figuring I had better get right to the point.

"I have heard. It's dreadful. You know his father and his grandfather died of heart attacks too."

"Really? But you know, it might not have been his heart."

"What do you mean?" she asked, her brows rising and eyes widening.

"There was a rather nasty blow to the back of his head. No way to tell until the autopsy if he had a heart attack and fell, hitting his head, or if he'd been hit and left there," I said bluntly. The shock registered in her blue eyes and she moved to a bench alongside the fire. I followed her and sat down. "Polly, what can you tell me about Darlene and Max, and their relationships with George?"

"What do you mean? Do you think they killed George!" Polly exclaimed.

"I have no idea, Polly, but I do know that if he was killed the police will suspect Alice. I want to find out who might have done it, to help her," I said.

Polly looked me in the eyes and nodded. "All right, I'll tell you what I know. Darlene seems to be thoroughly infatuated with George. He's her knight in shining armor. She was treading water just above the poverty level when they met. He brought her into a world of luxury and she'll never have to worry about money again. She has him on a pedestal and he loves it. Max, on the other hand, seems to hate his father more every year. He blames George for every problem he has and, at the same time, relies on George entirely as his sole support. Very sick."

"Alice said something about Max checking himself into a rehab program. Do you know anything about that?"

"Yes, George made a deal with Max. If Max stayed in a drug rehab program for six months, George would give him the three hundred thousand dollars Max wanted as a down payment on a beach house."

"Nice deal, fifty thousand a month!"

"Yes, isn't it! The way George figured it, Max would get the money someday anyway and if he could kick the drug habit, at least he'd have a chance of keeping what he'd inherit. If Max didn't straighten up soon, there was no way he'd survive."

"That bad?"

"That bad. It really bothered George but he didn't know what to do. The kid is thirty-four and should be responsible for himself. But he's never been very stable and after George divorced Max's mother, Max really started acting out. Max's never gotten past the divorce and George felt very guilty about it."

Not guilty enough to change his ways I thought, but kept that comment to myself.

"So, is Max in the rehab program now?" I asked.

"Yes. This is the middle of his second month."

"Where is this place? I assume it's a live-in facility?"

"Yes it is. It's in Laguna, south of LA."

"Did you see George a lot?"

"Oh, almost every week. We live— lived— next to each other in the city, you know."

"Do you like his new wife?"

"Like is a funny word. We don't have anything in common, but I've made my peace with the fact that she's George's new wife. So I'm nice to her for George's sake."

Ron reappeared too quickly with Polly's refilled champagne glass. The firelight shimmered on Polly's designer jacket as she took the glass from Ron's outstretched hand.

"Well, I'll leave you two to continue your conversation. I think I'll get a bite to eat. Thanks for the help, Polly," I said and made my way back towards the house.

Suddenly feeling exhausted and less like socializing, I decided to slip back home rather than go back into the party. I'd learned what I wanted to find out and I wanted to check in with Alice.

I made my way around the north side of the house and out to the front field/parking lot. The moon was full, helping me find my way on the uneven ground. As I came around to the front of the house I heard two male voices in heated conversation.

"You're up to a hundred grand now and I want it back by Friday."

"Right! And if I could pay you back by Friday I wouldn't be asking for twenty more now, would I?"

"Look, talk to your banker, your brother-in-law, who ever, but I don't want to be involved in this anymore! I want out!"

"You're in!" the other said, moving from the shadows of the tall evergreens lining the front of the house and walking toward the front door. The second figure ran after him and grabbed the other's right arm twisting it behind his back. I couldn't hear what they said now. Their voices were garbled with the sounds of the party and another car pulling into the drive. When they were on the porch and in the light, I recognized the two figures as Matt and Brad Bonner, two brothers who had moved their business and families out here about five years ago. Brad had a gambling habit that was no secret. My guess was he'd been borrowing from his brother to fund his gambling. As they went into the party, I made my way to my car and headed home.

Chapter
6

Late Night Calls

Walking in the door, I saw the message light blinking on my answering machine. On a Saturday night, I hadn't expected calls. Somehow, I didn't think the news would be good. I pressed the playback button and took off my jacket. Alice's voice filled the room. "Karen, I'm in the county jail. You are my one call. I'm not kidding. Please get over here! And call a lawyer!" Her voice cracked. "I'm scared." Then she hung up.

I heard a dial tone, a click, and the second message began: "Karen, it's Donald. The sheriff arrested Alice. We got back home around five and they were there waiting for her. They said they'd found a fire iron with blood on it in the stable and the prints on the handle match hers. The shape of the fire iron matches the blows on George's head. Call me. I went to the jail with her, but once they took her in, I came back here to find you."

My mind reeled.

The call had come in only twenty minutes ago. I called Donald at Alice's. It was eight-thirty now. Alice had been in jail for what, just over three hours. While I waited for Donald to answer the phone, I thought about calling Mark to get an attorney for Alice.

Mark Jordan is my friend, boyfriend, I guess you'd say, but the term sounds so juvenile, it doesn't quite fit our relationship. Mark has his own law firm in Chicago, where I used to practice law. Not at his firm, I mean in the city. We met at a Bar Association function. I'd just ended a long, tumultuous relationship and was not looking for another, but that's a story for another time. Mark and I have a relationship based on deep feelings and limited time. But we each know the other will be there if we need anything. And I definitely need help now. I've been out of the law practice for five years now and my contacts are cold. I'd have to rely on Mark's help to get a good criminal attorney for Alice. But first, I need to talk to Donald.

All this raced through my mind in the two rings it took for Donald to answer the phone.

"Donald, it's Karen."

"Karen, my God, I can't believe what's happening out here," Donald said. "This is crazy! Of course Alice didn't kill George, but the sheriff's people seem convinced she did! She's actually in a jail cell. They have her there until there's a bail hearing. Oh my God, I don't believe this!" Donald exclaimed again.

Donald had come out here for a quiet country weekend and ended up with his girlfriend in jail charged with murder. They'd only been dating for three months, so his ideas about Alice were probably still evolving. This was surely hard to fit in with anything he knew about her so far.

"Donald, I'm coming over and getting some things together for Alice. She'll need clothes, toiletries, something to read or do until we can get her out of there on Monday."

"Monday!" The shock in his voice told me he'd expected to get her out tomorrow, or maybe even tonight. I didn't think that would be possible.

"Yes. I don't think we can get a hearing on Sunday and anyway, we need to get a lawyer for her. I think we'll want to bring in someone from Chicago. I'll call Mark as soon as we hang up and then I'll be over."

"Good. I'll be waiting for you."

I could hear the relief in his voice that he hadn't expressed in words. This was Donald's first visit to Alice's and of course the haunted house stories on top of this murder would give anyone the creeps, even a six foot four, two hundred and ten pound former football player like Donald. I invited him to spend the night in my guest house. It was the least I could do and it would probably be more convenient if we were going to be working together to get Alice out of jail.

I pressed the end button on the phone and speed dialed Mark's home. He usually works late, but Saturday night at eight-thirty I expected even Mark to be home. He answered on the third ring.

"Mark, it's me."

"Karen! Hi, what a nice surprise. I thought you were at a country fete this evening."

"I was there for awhile. It's been an unusual day, to say the least, and I headed home early. Then when I got here there was a message for me from Alice. She's in trouble and called for my help."

"What's the matter?

"Well, that's why I'm calling. I do need your help."

"Sure, what's the problem?"

"Alice has been arrested."

"Arrested! For what?"

"For murder."

"Murder! What are you talking about?"

"Alice found George Almonte's body lying by her pond this morning. The police have arrested Alice for his murder. They have her in jail here in Galena."

"Whoa, that is way too fast! There couldn't have been much of an investigation."

"I know, and things usually move at ultra slow speed out here. It took five years for the city to put a public restroom in the Visitors' Center—and this is a tourist town! But, there's an election coming up in a few weeks and I think the sheriff figured he needed an unsolved murder in this quiet little burg like he needed a hole in the head. But a solved murder, now that could be his ticket to victory."

"Yes, if the case is solved correctly. But he has to be jumping the gun here, unless he has a smoking gun. Any guns involved here?" Mark loved playing with words, puns, double entendres. Usually this made conversing with him fun. But I was in no mood for jokes just now.

"Mark, this is not funny. And no, there was no gun involved. George had a gash on his head and was lying there by the pond. I don't know how the sheriff can even be sure it wasn't a heart attack, except of course for the fire iron—so, he probably was killed by the blow," I said, thinking out loud.

"Let's get back to Alice. Why did they arrest her?" Mark asked.

"They said they found her fingerprints on the handle of a fireplace iron hidden in the barn. Apparently, there was blood on the tip of the fire iron and the shape of the fire iron matched the blow on George's head."

"Hmm, what does Alice have to say about that?"

"I haven't spoken to her since they found the weapon. She said she noticed it was missing this morning."

"What do you want me to do?"

"Find a good criminal lawyer to get Alice out of jail as soon as possible which, I suppose, is going to be Monday," I said.

"It is Saturday night, but I'll give Frank Bonafiglio a call. He'd be great if he can take the case. Last I saw him he was getting ready for the Hillborough trial but that was a month ago. I'll let you know when I reach him."

"Thanks, Mark," I said, relaxing slightly with the knowledge that help was on the way.

"Karen, fill me in on time frames and what you know about George's death."

I gave him the little I knew: George's call about the horse documents, Alice's driving up Friday night as usual, and then finding George's body Saturday morning.

"Does Alice have any ideas about who might have killed George?" he asked.

"We haven't had a chance to talk about it too much. I'm on my way down to the jail to see her and I'll ask her more about that."

"Bring someone with you. I don't like the idea of your going there alone," he said.

"I'll bring Donald. I think he'd like the company as much as I would."

"Good idea. Well, let me get going on calling Frank. I'll get back to you. Keep your cell phone on."

"I will, but if I'm driving, you may not be able to get through. The hills on Blackjack Road block the signal. I'll check my messages as soon as I get into town."

"Karen, be careful."

"I will. And I'll have Donald with me."

"All right. I love you—I'll talk to you as soon as I reach Frank."

"I love you too. And Mark, thank you. I'll call you after I've talked to Alice, if we haven't connected before then."

"Okay. That's a plan."

I said, "Good bye" and we hung up.

I filled my water bottle to take with me for the drive. I don't think clearly if I'm dehydrated, so I am constantly carrying water with me.

I put the filled bottle in my purse, grabbed my coat, and headed out the door.

Even though Alice is my dear friend, I still hate going to her house and alone at night is really the worst. I think Donald must have felt the same way. He had his coat on and was waiting for me. We went up to Alice's bedroom together and I threw a night gown, two fresh changes of clothes, tooth brush and toothpaste, facial cream and makeup in the bag I'd brought with me.

Donald already had his overnight bag in his car, so he followed me back the seven miles to my place. We dropped off his car and headed out again in mine.

Chapter 7

Go Directly to Jail

It was nine-thirty at night by the time we arrived at the jail.

Galena's municipal buildings were constructed of limestone blocks, hand hewn by the miners who'd come in search of their fortunes in the 1830's. They spent their days slumped in four foot mine shafts, chiseling through dirt and stone, breathing sooty stale air. But a solid strike could change their fortunes. The many mansions around town stand as a monument to the success of that era. Fortunately or unfortunately, depending upon your point of view, the lead and steamboating industries nearly evaporated about 1860, train lines bypassed Galena, and the town fell into a hundred year sleep. Today, as a tourist town, Galena's spirit is firmly rooted in that era of past glory.

We climbed the large stone stairs and went through the oversized carved wooden doors. A single officer in uniform sat behind the long dark counter. She was the dispatcher and the deputy on duty. We stood there for a minute before getting her attention.

"Hello. We're here to see Alice Almonte. She was brought here a few hours ago."

"I'll check," the officer said and moved back to her desk. She spoke on the phone to someone for a minute and then said we could go on down. She pointed to a stairway and told us to walk down one level to the jail.

As we exited the stairway, we found ourselves in another small room. At one end of this room was a reception counter with a uniformed officer behind it. He was looking at us as we walked up to the counter.

"Hello, I am Karen Prince and this is Donald Strong. We're here to see Alice Almonte." I gave him my best smile, hoping he'd conclude that we were Alice's friends and not accomplices in crime.

"Visiting hours aren't until Sunday at ten."

"Can't we please see her? I brought her some clean clothes for tomorrow. What can it hurt?"

He looked at us appraisingly and apparently decided we weren't going to stage a jail break. "All right, I suppose," he said and opened the door to the right of the reception counter. "Follow me. You can see her for fifteen minutes. But I'll have to search the bag you have there, Ms. Prince."

"Of course," I said, holding the gym bag out to him.

The officer placed the bag on the counter and unpacked the clothes I had carefully folded. He opened the makeup kit, examined the skin cream, and pronounced the items all right to bring in.

As he was stuffing the clothes back in the bag, I stepped forward and offered assistance, hoping to intervene before the creases he was creating became permanent. I wanted Alice to look as good as possible when she went in for her bond hearing.

"I can do that for you," I said, as I reached for the white cotton blouse.

After I repacked Alice's clothes, we followed the officer into a small room. The room was bare except for two tables with four plastic chairs around each. The officer motioned us to the first table and said he'd be back in a few minutes.

He returned with Alice, who was wearing hand cuffs. It was a shock to see her looking so frightened. The steel cuffs on her wrists brought home the danger she was in if we didn't find the real murderer quickly.

"I'll be back in fifteen minutes," the officer said, leaving the three of us in the small stone walled room.

"I brought you fresh clothes for tomorrow," I said and put the bag I'd brought on the edge of the table.

"Thanks. I guess that means you can't get me out of here tonight, huh?"

"I don't think so," I said, unbidden tears welling in my eyes. I knew she must be frightened, and I was feeling very helpless and a bit frightened myself at the moment.

"But Mark is making calls as we speak to find you a good lawyer. With luck, your lawyer will be out here tomorrow and get you out of here Monday."

Her eyes grew large, taking in the sentence of another full day and night in jail. But she said, "Thanks. I appreciate everything you're doing for me."

Then she turned her attention to Donald. "Heck of a weekend in the country I've got you into Donald—sorry."

"Sorry? You don't have to be sorry, Alice. This isn't your fault. I'm just sorry you have to go through this. I'll make arrangements with my secretary tomorrow to cancel my appointments on Monday. I'll be here to help straighten this out."

"You don't have to do that," Alice said, but you could see the hope in her eyes. Our presence was clearly a lifeline for her.

"We only have ten more minutes here," I said. "We need your help. You need to seriously think about who might have done this."

"I haven't thought about anything else. And I don't know how we can ever know."

"We'll know," I said, putting more confidence into the words than I felt at the moment. "Just give us something to get started on. What's your best guess?"

"Okay," she said, taking a deep breath and exhaling audibly. "Check out that little witch George married. She is such a gold digger. She only married George for his money. Maybe she just didn't want to wait. Or maybe she got back together with her muscleman boyfriend and George was going to divorce her."

"She had a boyfriend?" I asked. I was surprised. Alice hadn't mentioned this before, but then, she hadn't talked much about this painful subject to me, or anyone else, I suspected.

"Well, she did before she stole George from me," Alice said. "Maybe she never really broke up with him and they planned to get rid of George together. I wouldn't put it past her," Alice added.

"Calm down Alice. What's the name of this boyfriend?"

"David Canter. He works at Gold Coast Health Club. He's a personal trainer there."

"He's still there do you think?"

"Last I heard he was."

"Great. I'll check it out—find out if they are still seeing each other, what their relationship is."

"What about George's partner, Richard Fox?" I asked. "Did you know him well?"

31

"Sure did," Alice said. "We did everything together during the early years of our marriage. Rich and George worked very closely together. And Marge and I had dinner together whenever the guys traveled. The four of us vacationed together, even celebrated holidays together. Yes, I knew him pretty well. But I haven't seen them for almost seven years now. After George and Rich had their falling out, it was awkward between Marge and me. There was too much we couldn't talk about. Seemed strained, and we gradually just lost touch."

"What was the problem between George and Rich?"

"It started as a business disagreement, I think. George didn't talk to me much about it. Just said they couldn't agree on how to run the businesses anymore, but it seemed like there was more to it. They'd handled business differences before, but George's attitude changed. He stopped trusting Rich. Wouldn't tell him things, thought Rich was taking advantage of the company."

"Such as?" I prompted.

"Oh, generally going over the top on expenses. George said Rich didn't seem to care anymore about making a profit, he was just spending money as fast as he could."

"They still had some businesses together didn't they?"

"I don't know what they've done since my divorce. When I left they had only two of the businesses left jointly, and those were for sale. They'd divided everything else up."

"Any reason that Rich would want George out of the way?"

"Not that I know of, but that doesn't mean anything. As we now know, George certainly didn't tell me everything when we were married." She raised one eyebrow.

"Anything else you think I should check out?"

"Well, you should probably find out where Max was. He's been calling me for the last six months, complaining about his father. Guess he was looking for a sympathetic ear."

"Didn't you tell me the other day that Max was in a rehab program? What facility is he in?"

"Oh, let me think. I know it's south of Laguna Beach, on the California coast. Some fancy place, expensive as heck I'm sure. Wait, it's—oh, I think it's called Beachhead or something like that. I remember it sounded like a resort and I'm sure it looks like one too."

"Do you think Max would have done this? Killed his father, I mean?"

"I guess I don't think he did. I know he's confused, but I don't think he'd go so far as to kill George. Still, someone did, so let's just see where he was at the time. If you find out he was in the rehab center, then that'll take him out of the picture."

"Is there anything else we can do for you until we can get you out of here?" I asked.

"Oh Karen, you're already doing so much. I don't want to get you involved in this mess."

"If you're involved, I'm involved. We're sisters right?" I asked. We weren't blood sisters. We'd chosen each other as sisters years ago and the bond was stronger than any other friendship I'd ever experienced.

"Right," she said and managed a smile. "You'll have to call Brenda and let her know what's happened. Tell her I won't be in the gallery on Monday—and maybe not all week. If people call about—this, she should just say she doesn't know anything. Ask her to cancel my appointments through Friday. She should keep the gallery open the usual hours. If anything comes up she can't handle, she should email me and I'll check my messages. Oh, Karen, you'll have to check my messages for me and let me know what they are. Just print them out. You know my email address; my password is buyart."

"Buyart?" I asked.

"Yes, that's what I'm buying now that the stock market has gone to hell in a hand basket. But I guess this weekend puts that in perspective, doesn't it?"

"Yes, sort of dwarfs what we thought were our big problems. Well, we'll get this straightened out. Then at least you'll be out of here." We managed a smile.

Donald squeezed her hand across the table. "I'll see you tomorrow," he said.

"I'll be here," she said with a weary smile.

We arrived back at my place about eleven. I showed Donald the guest cabin, made a fire in the fireplace for him, and left him to settle in and get some rest.

At home, I took off my jacket and saw the red message light flashing again. I remembered that I had forgotten to check my cell phone. Mark had called just twenty minutes ago. His message said Frank Bonofiglio would be out here tomorrow afternoon. Legal help was on the way.

Chapter 8

Trip to Town

I woke up to the orange dawn light glowing in my east bedroom windows. Truffs weighted my ankles. I slipped my feet from under her and I rolled to my right to check the clock: six am. I needed to be here until Frank arrived, but then it seemed I could do more good in the city than out here. Frank would get Alice out of jail as quickly as possible. In the meantime I needed to check out Darlene, her ex-boyfriend, and Max and Rich's whereabouts Friday night.

I made my way downstairs, poured myself a cup of freshly brewed coffee and sent a mental thank you to the inventor of the timed electric coffee maker. I poured milk into the steaming black liquid and took that first wonderful sip. Truffs had followed me downstairs and was sitting in front of the pantry door staring at it. I got the picture. She wanted her breakfast. I eased the door open, moving slowly so as not to disturb Her Highness, and grabbed her morning can of Fancy Feast. I placed the saucer of sliced turkey in front of her and Truffs trilled in appreciation before beginning her petite dejunier.

It was too early to call Mark, so I started up my laptop and searched for rehab institutes near Laguna. Google gave me three possibilities: The Beachfront, The Kramer Institute, and the Tellings Foundation. I figured the Beachfront to be the one Alice meant when she said the Beachhead. I put the info in a folder in my laptop and wrote the main number in the little notebook I carry in my purse. I created a file on my computer for each of the suspects. Looking in the Chicago yellow pages I found the name, address, and phone number for the Gold Coast Health Club Alice had mentioned. It was located a bit north and west of the technical boundaries of the Gold Coast area, but the name carried enough cache that merchants used it if they were anywhere within a mile of the actual Gold Coast. The address put it about three blocks from George's home. Their ad said they were open 24/7, so I called and booked an appointment for ten-thirty Monday morning with my new trainer, David Canter. That would give me a leisurely morning with Mark.

I went back upstairs and dressed for my morning run. I put in three miles, three times a week, just like the doctors ordered. It always felt good when I was done, and sometimes even when I was doing it. Today I decided to go cross country. A red tailed hawk circled overhead and screeched as I crossed his hunting territory. The crisp air felt good. I lost myself in the effort of the jog, my own breathing and the crunch of leaves beneath my feet the only other sounds.

When I got back, I did my stretches, and then called Mark. He sounded wide awake and I was glad he was up early. We made arrangements to meet for dinner tonight at La Lista, the newest of the upscale restaurants Mark favored. Mark said Frank would be here at ten, which gave me only two hours to shower, dress, and pack. I had to get going. We said goodbye and I called Louise. Thank heavens for Louise and Tony. They would watch Truffles and take care of the house while I was in the city figuring out what happened to George.

I took a quick shower, and then stood in my closet considering my wardrobe choices. Years ago I'd developed the habit of dressing for the high point of my day. This usually results in my being over dressed for a portion of the day, but I really don't care. I like my dressy clothes and I'm definitely not going to waste time changing twice in one day. So I slipped into my sexiest red Donna Karen sheath dress and topped it with a black Miyake jacket to tone it down for the daytime. I put on black flats in the name of safety and threw my three inch heels in a bag for the front seat of the Boxster. There is no back seat. I didn't need toiletries since I was planning to stay at Mark's—hmm. But I did need a businesslike outfit for Monday. I rolled a black St. John's skirt and top and put that in my leather brief case. The brief case served as my overnight travel bag but looked so much more business like walking into restaurants.

Well, I was ready to go. Now to be sure Donald knew the game plan. I knocked loudly on the guest cabin door, but found Donald already up and sitting in the screened-in porch. I gave him the detailed map of Galena that I kept in the information drawer in the guest cabin. I asked him to explain to Alice that I was going to the city to see what I could learn to help her. I told Donald that Frank would be here shortly and I would give them the use of my office in the walk out level of my house. Donald offered to drive Frank to the jail to see Alice, which would work out perfectly. I gave Donald my cell number and asked him to let me know if there was anything he or Frank needed while they were here. I gave him Louise and Tony's number, as well as Mark's phone number, secretly hoping they wouldn't call this evening. Life is short. "Pick yee rose buds while yee may" —or something like that.

We poured ourselves cereal for breakfast and spent the next few minutes getting to know each other a bit more while crunching whole grain flakes. Donald told me he was in the middle of getting city council approval for another hotel on the Magnificent Mile. This one, as the others already in existence, would have retail shops on the first six levels, office space on the next twenty floors, and luxury condominiums on the top thirty floors. The unique feature of this building would be a central park-like courtyard on the top of the structure for residents' use only. Donald had parlayed his name recognition from his football days into goodwill for his development projects. He seemed to be able to get approvals for everything he undertook, which is unusual in the highly political arena of Chicago real estate development.

My cell phone rang as we were finishing breakfast. It was Frank and he was just turning onto Blackjack. I said I'd meet him at the house and left Donald to get ready for his day.

Frank drove up in a black Mercedes. Black is not a country color for a car, too much dust on the roads, but then, Frank was not usually a country lawyer. He was of medium height, with dark hair, intelligent bright eyes, and a quick smile that worked well with judges and juries alike. I thanked Frank for coming out to help Alice and explained my plans for the next few days in the city. I showed Frank his office/bedroom suite and then took him to the guest house and introduced him to Donald. The two of them seemed to hit it off quickly and I felt comfortable leaving Alice in the hands of these two capable fellows.

With apologies for my quick departure, I exchanged phone numbers with Frank and took my leave.

The country portion of the drive from Galena to Chicago makes the whole drive worthwhile. The rolling hills, tended farm fields and the fall colors were beautiful and calming. I drifted from conscious appreciation of the vistas to the meditative state that driving induces. In the middle of this shift my mind produced a streaming list of things I need to do.   I keep a pocket size tape recorder on the passenger seat to record these "to do" thoughts as they come to mind. Home items popped up first: pay real estate taxes, order spring plants for the garden, make an appointment for Truffs' annual shots.   Once this stream has passed, I often have some exciting insights.   Some of my best painting ideas have come to me while I'm driving.   Today however, my mind focused on more pressing matters: how to approach Polly, Rich Fox, and David Canter.

Polly is a public relations specialist, so discussing my plans for Turning Points Foundation was a perfect reason to meet with her. This had the benefit of doing two things at once, which always gives me a sense of satisfaction. Guess I felt I was beating time, that indefatigable thief.   I'd see if Polly could meet with me first thing tomorrow morning.

Then there was Rich Fox. I tried on the idea of meeting with him to discuss investing some of my money in his business ventures, but I really didn't know enough about what he did to make that work. I decided to go with the direct approach and just ask him about his relationship with George.   If he hadn't already heard about the murder, I'd tell him and see his reaction.   But in all likelihood, George's death was already all over the Chicago papers.

With David, my intro would be easy. I'd tell him that Polly had mentioned his name at Saturday's party and that I was looking for a good body building program. I planned to set up a standing Monday morning appointment and make arrangements to call for additional sessions when business brought me to the city.

Getting information about Max would be harder. I'd have to fly out to California. The rehab facility would probably have strict rules about patient's privacy. Certainly they should. Ah, maybe Max will come out here for George's funeral, assuming there was going to be a service. That would be a good time to meet him. Well, maybe not a good time, but certainly an opportunity.   Polly would probably know more about the family arrangements. I decided to call her from the car.

I have a voice operated phone in the Boxster and asked it to dial 411. I'd gotten it for safety, but I also liked the 007 effect. The operator found Polly's country home number and connected the call for me. She answered on the third ring. "Polly, hi, it's Karen Prince."

"Hi, Karen! Good to see you last night. You just caught me before I left for the city. Where are you calling from? It sounds like you're in a wind tunnel."

"I'm heading into Chicago myself—calling from the car. I was hoping I'd catch you before you left. Seeing you last night gave me an idea. I was wondering if we could meet tomorrow morning at your office to talk about a public relations plan to introduce a foundation I'm setting up."

"Sure, that sounds interesting. I have a ten o'clock, but we could have an early meeting, say eight-thirty?"

So much for my leisurely morning with Mark. "That should work. You're at Three Thirty-Three aren't you?"

"Yes, thirty-fifth floor."

"Great. See you then. Oh, Polly, do you know if there are any arrangements for a funeral service for George?"

"Yes, I just spoke with Darlene. The family is planning on a service Thursday morning. It'll depend on the autopsy being done and the body being back in Chicago by Wednesday. But the sheriff told Darlene they should be able to release the body by Tuesday afternoon."

"Do you know where they're going to have the service?" I asked.

"At the funeral home on Elm and Dearborn. Darlene is having people back to the house afterward."

"Thanks, Polly. I'll see you tomorrow morning at eight-thirty."

"See you then," she said and rang off.

The rest of the drive was mercifully uneventful. The last time I'd driven into Chicago, a six foot long lead pipe had flown off the back of a truck rumbling down the highway ahead of me. The pipe had landed on the highway and I'd watched this potential tire deflator skitter across two lanes directly toward me. With cars on either side of me and one on my tail, I had no choice but to take my chances and drive over this rolling hazard. Luckily, I'd been in the Jeep, and had a bit more clearance over the road. I felt the bump, but the tires held. I heard horns blare and brakes screech as the cars behind me negotiated their way over or around the pipe. I'd gone to my service dealer when I'd gotten into the city. Luckily the pipe had hit a tie bar. The only permanent damage was to my driving peace of mind. I now check the cargo of the trucks in all lanes ahead of me and avoid trailing any trucks with open beds.

Being Sunday morning, there was less than the usual amount of traffic. The four lanes heading into the city were full but not stopped. That passes for light traffic these days on the toll road into Chicago.

Two o'clock. I'd made good time and decided to see if I could catch Mark at home. His condo was in a Mies building overlooking Lake Michigan. The rooms had floor to ceiling glass windows with views of Oak Street Beach to the north, the Lake due east, and Navy Pier to the south. The sunrises over the lake were some of the most glorious I've ever seen.

I parked in the underground garage and the doorman buzzed me into the building. Mark greeted me at his condo door with a kiss that said I'd definitely been on his mind. We had a few hours here before dinner and I couldn't think of a better way to spend them. I returned his kiss with open arms. I'd dropped my bag to the floor with the first embrace and now let my jacket shrug off my shoulders. Mark's kisses made their way down my neck. His lips caressed the bare skin along the spaghetti straps of my dress. His hands on either side of my waist, he pulled me into him. I loved the feel of him, the scent of him. I was floating in a world where there were only the two of us and an urgent passionate need to be as close as possible. Suddenly clothes were barriers. His hands moved the zipper in the back of my dress and I unbuckled his belt.

We surfaced from this other world two hours later, laying softly in each other's arms. He looked into my eyes and whispered, "Hello." I smiled and answered, "Hello."

We made our way into the shower. Mark's marble clad shower was an experience—sort of the surround sound version of showers. Nine jets of water came from the ceiling and the walls. Mark kissed me again and we fell back into the whirl of lovemaking of reunited lovers. When we rejoined the world another hour had gone by, and it was time to get ready for dinner in earnest. Already in the shower, we added soap, scrubbed each other, and somewhat reluctantly dressed for dinner.

Mark poured us each a glass of Macallan's eighteen old year single malt scotch and brought out a plate of salmon and caviar. He made hot toast to serve them on and we settled into the sofa to talk about Alice. I told him of my appointments with Polly and David tomorrow morning and said I wanted to talk to Rich Fox tomorrow afternoon, although I didn't know if he would see me. At this point I could only go over my list of suspects with Mark. I really didn't have any leads and I was getting anxious to start my search to find George's killer. There wasn't anything I could do until tomorrow, except call Frank and see what progress he was making in Galena.

We reached Frank on his cell phone. He'd met with both Alice and the State's Attorney. Even though it was Sunday, the State's Attorney had come down to the jail when he heard that Alice's "lawyer from the city" had arrived. They'd come to agreement that Alice would be released on a one hundred thousand dollar bond on Monday morning. That, at least, was good news. I promised to fill Frank in about my meetings with David and Polly tomorrow afternoon.

Next we called Donald. He was at the guest house and said he'd spent the day with Alice. She was holding up as well as could be expected. He'd brought her email messages. Now that the Chicago papers had picked up the murder, people were calling and emailing her like crazy. Alice created an email letter to reassure the people writing her that this was all a tragic mistake and that she'd be back at her gallery shortly. She'd asked Donald to return her phone calls and deliver the same message.

Louise had checked on Donald and offered to bring him anything he needed. Donald and Frank were going out for dinner. I suggested they go to Eagle Ridge, the nearby golf resort, and have dinner at their restaurant. I felt guilty going out with Mark for a fabulous dinner while Alice was in jail. But my not having dinner wasn't going to get her out of there any faster, so on we went to La Lista.

The restaurant is only a four block walk from Mark's. On the corner of Oak and Michigan, La Lista is nestled between the office and residential floors of the marble clad building at the foot of the Mag Mile. Overlooking both the Beach and the lights of Michigan

Avenue, sitting in the glass enclosed bay windows was a premier experience. The restaurant was tiered, so that tables farther away from the windows still had a Lake and an Avenue view.

Sitting across from Mark, the candle light gave a warm glow to his eyes and a soft atmosphere to the restaurant. The sommelier brought the wine list and Mark selected a bottle of Tenuta di Ornello, a wonderful red wine we'd found while traveling in Venice last spring. We'd brought a bottle back for Vince, the owner of La Lista, and now they kept a case of this wine here especially for us.

We started with fresh roasted vegetables on a bed of polenta, topped with goat cheese. Then came the homemade spagettini con frutti di mare, followed by a fresh organic greens salad. The tiramisu—which literally translated means "lift me to heaven"—lived up to its name. Mark, the food, the setting, everything was perfect: a little pocket of paradise, just for the moment. But then, the moment is all we really ever have isn't it?

We walked home, arm in arm, looking in the windows at the glittering jewelry and designer clothes. The night air was brisk and I leaned into Mark. He put his arm around my shoulder and we walked the last few blocks to his place.

The eastern view in the bedroom made for early summer wake up calls as the sunlight streamed onto the bed and brightened the room. Now that fall was here, the sun rose later allowing us to sleep until seven.

We both moved quickly in the morning. Mark was in his running gear and out the door as I entered the shower. I was skipping the run this morning. I'd be walking at least an hour to my meetings today. And besides, I had a ten-thirty appointment with my new trainer.

I was out the door by seven forty-five, dressed and in need of coffee. I walked to the nearest Starbucks and bought a large cup with skim to go. The pace of the city hadn't changed since I'd left. The sidewalks still were filled with young professionals making their way to their offices. As I made my way down Michigan Avenue I checked out the store windows filled with fall clothing. The soft fabrics and muted colors were alluring. Still, as I passed store after store, I wondered where all the merchandise went? Here is a mile long strip of buildings with stores in every one, many of these buildings with seven or eight floors of stores. And this is just one shopping area in a city with thousands of shopping areas and malls. And this city is only one of thousands of cities with similar malls, each filled with merchandise. I marveled at the abundance.

The southern end of Mag Mile was bounded by the Chicago River. I crossed the bridge and was now in the Loop. The streets here are lined with office buildings and I began thinking of my meeting in a few minutes with Polly.

My goal would be to learn as much as possible about George, Darlene and Max. I'd have to do this while talking about my foundation. I'd start with a description of the foundation and then lead the conversation to George, Darlene, and Max. Polly would want to learn more about the foundation and wouldn't risk offending a new client, so I'd probably be able to learn whatever she might know about George and his family. I had my plan in place as I climbed the stairs to the green glass entry doors to Polly's office building.

Chapter
9

Interviews

I rode the packed elevator to the thirty-fifth floor. Looking up and down the hallway trying to decide which direction to go, I saw large glass doors at the far north end of the hall clearly marking a large office. It looked like Polly's style, so I headed in that direction. As I got closer, I read "Andrews Public Relations" stenciled in gold letters on the doors. Yes, this place was definitely Polly's. A sea foam green carpet echoed the color of the glass exterior of the building. There was a long sleek blonde wood reception desk just inside the front door. A magnificent six foot tall bouquet was centered against the wall of windows overlooking the River.

I gave my name to the young man at the desk and walked to the windows to wait. I could see three bridges spanning the river below. A cluster of sail boats gathered in front of the nearest bridge. I watched the long crossing arms drop across the bridge stopping car traffic. Lights at each end of the bridge blinked and the massive structure parted at its center, the two halves rising, pointing high into the air. Frustrated commuters, pedestrians and drivers alike, would have to wait as the bridge rose to allow the boaters to make their way up river to winter docks.

Before the bridge had begun to lower, a young woman in a lavender suit approached me. She introduced herself as Ann, Polly's secretary, and asked me to follow her.

The whole office was furnished in the same sleek blonde wood as the reception desk. The light colored wood and carpet and the glass exterior walls gave the space a feeling of light and air.

Polly was waiting for me behind her long immaculate desk. I never understood how people could get anything done and keep such a neat desk. I never could, and I admired the ability to delegate that it implied. Polly got up and gave me a hug. She was in a gorgeous pale blue Armani suit. If the elegant styling and fabric hadn't told me, I'd have known it was Armani simply because Polly was wearing it. He was her signature designer. We sat at a round marble table in the corner of her office. Sitting felt good. Even though I was in flats, the soles of these dress shoes provided only a fraction of the cushioning of my usual New Balance. Life in the Windy City had its costs and comfortable dressing was one of them. Ann brought us both coffee and water.

As we sipped the coffee, I introduced the subject of Turning Points. I laid out my concept for the new foundation.

"I'll put twelve and a half million in government bonds. The yearly interest will fund grants for midlife career transitions into the creative arts. I want winning a Turning Points Fellowship to lend a certain status—a mark of approval—to the change of career. Screening will have to be very thorough. I want recipients to be successful in their current field and driven to succeed in their new one." I was on my soapbox now. "Twenty years in a field chosen when you're twenty can be frustrating for a creative mind. But society expects professionals to stay in their profession for another twenty years. Sometimes this works out well—the career and the person grow in the same direction. Sometimes it doesn't. I want to give those people a hand in reshaping their careers, especially in making a transition into the arts."

Polly nodded. I don't think she herself felt what I was saying. But she'd seen some of her friends, including me, make a career change. So she knew the phenomena existed and why it was a cause close to my heart. Polly was one of the blessed who lived and breathed work that she loved. It was what made her good at it.

"We should start by creating a board of well respected professionals for the foundation. They'll not only lend guidance, they'll create prestige and acceptance for it. Then we'll place articles in the papers. Maybe send intro letters to the existing foundations in the city. When will the first awards be granted?" Polly asked.

"I hope we'll be in a position to award them this time next year. I still need to get the foundation legally established and then we'll need to get the word out so we attract the right candidates," I said.

"What'll the award be?"

"A five year grant. During the five years I figure they'll need to study their chosen field for three years, then two years to get their feet on the ground and get established in their new fields."

"That's very generous," Polly said.

"I want this to be a complete transitional help so the candidates don't have to worry about where their living will come from year to year."

"How many recipients will you have each year?"

"I haven't set a number yet. Partly, that will depend on what I have to pay in administrative expenses: directors' fees, attorneys' fees, office overhead. I want the foundation to preserve principal and spend its earnings of about one million per year. If expenses are twenty-five percent, I'll have seven hundred and fifty thousand a year in grant money. So, maybe we'll have ten recipients per year. Maybe fewer in the first few years until we get the system established. "

"Sounds like a great concept. I'm sure you'll have lots of interesting candidates. Let me give some thought to recommendations for you for board members," Polly said.

I wasn't wild about the idea of having to deal with board members I didn't know, but I figured I'd listen to Polly's ideas and come to my own conclusions about that later.

"Thanks," I said. "I'm not thinking of a large board. I'd like to chair it myself, but a few outside directors are probably a good idea." I paused and then said, "It's really a shock about George, isn't it?" Not a graceful transition, but we were running low on time.

"That's an understatement! I've never even known anyone involved in a serious crime and then to have my neighbor murdered!"

"Have you spoken to Darlene?" I asked.

"Oh, yes! She's extremely upset, as you can imagine. She said George left for the stable for his usual ride Friday afternoon about two and just never came home. She called the police about ten, but they said they couldn't do anything for twenty-four hours. And then she got the call from the Galena Sheriff Saturday morning. It's all just horrible!"

"So George was in Chicago at two on Friday. It's a four hour drive from Chicago to Galena on Friday afternoon, so the soonest he could have been there was six. And it seems unlikely that he'd have said he was going to the horse stable and then driven out there."

"He didn't take his car. It's still in the garage," Polly said. "Darlene told me that."

"Darlene was home all Friday afternoon?" I asked.

"That's what she said. She said she started to wonder where he was about six. She thought he'd be home about five, but figured he'd stopped to do some shopping. When he still wasn't home two hours later, she started to worry. She stayed home in case he called."

"Was she home alone?" I asked.

"I think she was. She doesn't seem to have any close friends. It's usually just the two of them going out to dinner, or doing things," Polly said.

"What about David Canter? Are they still friends?" I asked.

Polly's eyebrows went up. I knew Polly and I knew she loved gossip. "Well, I think they still see each other on occasion. And she still works out at Gold Coast. I don't know why George didn't put a stop to that. Except that she did seem to get whatever she wanted from George. He was really so nuts about her. I don't think Darlene could do anything wrong in his eyes."

"Do you think she was still having an affair with Canter?"

"I don't really know—but she never did stop seeing him, I do know that."

"What's this Canter like? What do you hear about him?"

"Never met the fellow myself, though I have seen him once or twice, coming and going from George and Darlene's." Polly's eyebrows went up again, implying what she hadn't said directly.

"Really? When was that?"

"Oh, I see him about once a month. In fact, he was there last week," Polly said.

"Was George there then?"

"I'd suspect not," she said.

"But you don't know?"

"Well, I wouldn't really know. I just saw him coming in and out the Sunday afternoon before last and I think that's when George is usually riding. But of course, I could be wrong," she said.

"Did you know the police have Alice in jail?" I asked.

"I heard," Polly said. "She was really upset with George about the divorce. I don't think she ever got over it. She can't seem to talk about anything else when we see each other. Her pain is so palpable––but I didn't expect this," Polly said.

"You think she did it!" I said, rather taken aback. It hadn't occurred to me that anyone who knew Alice could think that. Polly looked serious. "Really? I can't see that," I said. There was a moment of silence which Polly quickly filled with back pedaling.

"No, no. You're right, I'm sure she didn't. I just meant I could see how the police could have made that assumption," she said.

I nodded. "I'd better get going. I have a ten o'clock and it's nine-thirty already."

"I'll call you in a few days with ideas for your Board and an introduction plan."

"Thanks, that'd be great, Polly."

"Will I see you at Darlene's on Thursday?" she asked.

"Yes, I'll be there. What time does it start?"

"The service is from two to four at Drakes Funeral Home. Then people are going to Darlene's house afterward."

"Thanks, I'll see you there if we don't talk before that."

We said goodbye and Ann appeared to escort me to the main entrance.

As we walked through the office I kept thinking of Polly's comments about Alice. I had no idea other people, besides the Galena detectives I mean, saw Alice as capable of George's murder. This did not bode well.

Chapter 10

Gold Coast

On the street, I hailed a taxi and headed to my ten o'clock. I'd already packed my gym clothes in my briefcase, so I asked the driver to take me directly to Clark and Oak.

Set at the western edge of one of the wealthiest sections of Chicago, Gold Coast Health Club was the latest in upscale workout facilities. The entry rivaled the lobby of a Michigan Avenue four star hotel. There were four people behind the reception counter to check in guests as they arrived. A waterfall cascaded through a three story glass tube in the center of the lobby. The far wall was a ten story climbing wall. A sports clothing boutique, a coat check room, and a restaurant completed the first floor. I checked in at the front desk, and then took the golden plexiglass stairs up one level to the ladies locker rooms. A bank of three elevators offered an alternative route to the upper floors where there were tennis, racquet ball, and squash courts, two running tracks, a swimming pool, and various exercise equipment rooms.

The dressing room was bright with polished white marble and stained white wood lockers. Gold carpet with the Gold Coast logo woven into a pattern ran through the hallways. I changed into my black top and Capri tights and went in search of the exercise machine room. I found it on the third level. The floor was covered in the same custom gold logo carpeting. The room was ringed with mirrors and filled with the latest equipment. There was a young woman sitting at a desk along one wall. I figured she kept track of appointments, so I introduced myself and asked if she knew where I could find David Canter. She suggested I warm up on one of the bicycles and said David would find me in a few minutes. She smiled, then picked up her phone and paged him.

I climbed on a treadmill and adjusted the headphones to tune in CNN. Each machine had its own set of headphones which could be tuned in to one of the three large televisions or one of the music stations.

I'd put in about five minutes when a dark, muscular, thirty-something man with shoulder length hair approached me. He put out his hand and flashed a bright wide smile. I pulled off my headphones in time to hear his introduction, "Hi, I'm David. You must be Karen."

"I am," I said as I climbed off the machine.

"So Karen, tell me, what brings you here today?"

"I'd like to start a training program and I hear you're an excellent trainer."

"Ah, who's talking about me like that?" he asked with a smile.

"A neighbor of George Almonte."

I watched his face closely but saw no obvious changes at the mention of George's name.

"Are you a friend of George's?" he asked.

"We were neighbors in Galena before his divorce." I paused, and then said, "Ah—have you heard what happened to him?"

"Yes," he said. "I saw it on the news—what a shocker."

"It was. And I'm trying to find out who could have done this."

"Really?" he said, his eyes widened. "The news said the police arrested his ex-, what's her name—Alice."

"They did, but she's a friend of mine and I know she didn't kill him," I said, somewhat defensively on Alice's behalf.

"And who do you think did?" he asked, looking me directly in the eye.

"I don't know, but that's what I want to find out," I said, meeting his stare.

"Well, I can't help you there. I didn't know the man," he said, and turned away.

I moved in front of him and said, "Didn't he work out here before he was married?"

"Yes, but I wasn't his trainer," he said dismissively.

"I heard Darlene was," I said.

"That's right," he said.

"And I heard that you were dating Darlene before she left you for George," I said, again looking for some reaction.

"It was nothing serious between Darlene and me. And it was over before she took up with George," he said.

"I heard you still see her," I said.

"What? Who said that?" he asked pointedly.

"What does that matter? Is it true? Are you still seeing Darlene?" I pressed on.

"No! Not like you mean," he said.

"One of the neighbors said you were visiting Darlene the weekend before last," I said.

"So what—are you here to spy on me? You have neighbors spying on me?" He spat the words.

"I am not spying on you. I'm trying to find out who killed George."

"Well, it wasn't me! And I think this training session is over," he said and stormed away.

I followed him again. "Hey, wait! I'm not accusing you. And the police will be asking you the same questions. So why not talk to me so I can get to the bottom of this?"

He looked me in the eyes for a long moment. His stare was dark and angry. "Look, I didn't have anything to do with this guy. Darlene called me sometimes to talk, that's all. She needed someone to talk to sometimes, and she turned to me. End of story."

"And what did she have to talk about the Sunday before last? You're going to have to tell the police anyway—" I said, encouragingly.

He paused for a moment and then said, "Just the usual—she's lonely. They were happy that first year. They each had their dream come true. He had a hot young lover; she had her sugar daddy. But time went by and she got bored because they don't have that much in common. He liked horses and art. She likes dancing and working out. So she invites me over every now and then for a beer and a laugh, but that's it."

"And why do you go?"

"She's an old friend, you know. We were together for two years. I don't turn my back on my friends."

"So you weren't upset when she took up with George?"

"No, I already told you, our thing was over by then."

I figured that was probably true. The question was whether they had separated by agreement to clear the way for Darlene to go after George or if they had really broken up.

51

"So, is that all you came here for, to ask me about George and Darlene?"

"No," I said, my fingers crossed behind my back. "I really want to set up a work out program."

"And you're coming all the way into the city just for your workouts?"

"Well, I come into the city fairly regularly. I thought we could arrange a weekly appointment. I hear you're really great, and I'll just work out at home on the other days." I find flattery never hurts, even with tough guys.

"Well, that's not how I usually work, but since you live so far away, guess we could try it."

"Great, so let's get started," I said with an enthusiastic smile. But I wondered why he hadn't just thrown me out. I didn't think he was desperate for clients in a place like this, so maybe he figured it was a good way to keep track of me. Great, so we'd be working each other for information while we worked out.

An hour later I was sweaty and sore and we agreed to meet at the same time and place next week.

In the locker room I made a mental note to check out our boy David's background and hit the showers. I had time for a steam and it felt great on my tired muscles.

Dressed and hungry, I stopped at the restaurant on the first floor for a quick salad. I ordered then pulled out my cell phone and called Rich Fox's office to make an appointment for this afternoon. His secretary told me that Rich was in town and could see me at one-thirty if I could hurry over. I was surprised to get in to see him so quickly. I wondered if his business was that slow, or if he knew I was a friend of Alice's and wanted to see what he could learn about George's murder. I guessed I'd find out shortly.

I called Frank Bonafiglio's cell phone but got his voice mail and left a message to call me. I'd hoped to hear that he had Alice free by now, but I guess he was working on it. The waiter brought out the salad I'd ordered and I dove in. I was starving.

Chapter 11

The Fox's Den

I finished lunch and made my way through the marble lobby to the line of waiting taxis. Getting a taxi is never a problem here. There is a steady stream of well to do exercisers coming and going from their offices to this workout wonderland. Rich Fox's office is in the Hancock Building, just a five minute taxi ride away. I'd been thinking of ways to approach him all the while I was crunching lettuce, but nothing clever had come to mind. In the taxi, I thought through the list of people we had in common, and tried to get a finger hold on a conversation that would enlighten me about Rich and George's history. But as I walked through the Hancock's revolving doors, I decided I would simply be straight forward. If he had nothing to hide, this shouldn't be a problem. If he did, I hoped I'd be sensitive enough to pick up on his discomfort or maybe catch him in an outright lie. I rode the bank of elevators to the twentieth floor and followed the hallway to the mahogany door labeled "Richard J. Fox Enterprises" in brass letters.

The receptionist greeted me and asked me to have a seat. There was no view here. Two upholstered chairs in deep red and gold tones sat across from the receptionist. A small cherry wood table stood in front of them and a gold rimmed mirror hung on the wall behind them. The table was empty—no magazines or flowers to distract me. So I watched the receptionist who seemed to be slowly folding and inserting a stack of letters into envelopes. The phones were quiet. Apparently Richard did not receive many visitors here.

In a few minutes, a sixty-something year old woman in a tailored suit came to greet me. She introduced herself as Jane Tyler, Mr. Fox's secretary, and escorted me back to Mr. Fox's private office. We walked by two rooms furnished as private offices, one of which was empty, the other occupied by a young man in his twenties. Jane walked into the next room and I followed her. The room was quite large with floor to ceiling windows looking out on Michigan Avenue.

This was Richard Fox's personal office and meeting room. There were two chairs in front of his desk, one of which Ms. Tyler offered me. Surprisingly, she sat in the other. There was a sofa against the wall opposite the desk, which I assumed provided additional seating for larger meetings. Or maybe it was where Mr. Fox took his afternoon nap. This place definitely seemed quiet enough for sleeping. I wondered how much work Richard Fox actually did these days.

Richard Fox began the conversation saying: "So, Ms. Prince, you asked to meet with me. What can I do for you?"

"First, thank you for meeting with me on such short notice Mr. Fox," I said.

"Please, call me Richard."

"Richard then. As I was saying, thank you. I assume you've heard that George Almonte was killed last Friday evening," I said.

"Yes, I've seen the news reports," he said.

"Well, I'm here because Alice Almonte, a dear friend of mine, and an old friend of yours, is accused of his murder. The police have arrested Alice. They're looking for a quick, simple answer and they've settled on her," I said.

I felt both Richard and Jane stiffen and saw them exchange glances.

"I'm sorry for Alice," Richard said. "We were friends for many years and I'd be happy to help her. But still I have to ask, what is it that you think I can do for you?"

"I'd like to know more about George and his business. I know Alice didn't kill him and I am trying to figure out who else might have."

"And you think it might be me?" he asked with a laugh in his voice. Jane did not seem to see the humor in this. She sat there, unmoving, looking at me.

"No, I am not suggesting in any way that you were involved in his murder. I'm only trying to learn more about George's business. One of my neighbors told me that you were partners with George for many years—going back to law school and that you parted ways about six or seven years ago. Is that right?"

"You've been doing your homework, I see. Yes, George and I graduated from law school together. We were best of friends in school and decided to start our law practice together when we graduated. We opened a small office near the federal courts and soon found ourselves with an active bankruptcy practice. After a while, we could see that people were buying bankruptcy assets for pennies on the dollar. And we got the idea to buy some of the businesses, the ones we felt we could turn around. George stopped practicing law and concentrated on finding assets to purchase and manage. We already knew most of the bankruptcy trustees, so it was just a matter of letting them know we were interested purchasers. These things are published in the Daily Law Bulletin you know, so anyone can bid on them."

"So you bought businesses together?"

"Yes, for many years. I kept up my bankruptcy law practice and George managed the businesses. I did the legal work for the businesses as well."

"Alice tells me you and George had a falling out and divided up your assets. Why was that?"

"Oh, I just wanted to retire, nothing more than slowing down really. I tired of the fight. George wanted to keep going. I didn't want to take the risk of buying anymore and so we sold what we could and divided up the rest. Nothing to make me want to kill George I'm afraid," he said and laughed again.

"I didn't mean to accuse you in coming here. I'm really only trying to get some history."

"Well, I hope I've been helpful," he said and rose to signify the end of our conversation.

"Yes, thank you."

Jane was on her feet by now as well. I shook hands with Richard and followed Jane back to the reception area.

"Have you been with Mr. Fox a long time, Jane?" I asked, trying to establish some rapport with her.

"From the beginning," she said. "Over thirty-five years together now."

I sensed Jane played a kind of protective role with her employer. They seemed more like partners than boss and secretary, but I guess they would be partners after thirty-five years. I wished the hall was longer so I'd have more time to explore their relationship and what Jane knew of George, but we were quickly at the reception desk.

"Thank you, Jane. Here's my card. If you think of anything I should know I'd appreciate your calling me. My cell number is on there, so even if I am in the city you'll be able to reach me."

"Thank you. I'll give it to Mr. Fox."

"I would appreciate that. And here is another card for you." I wasn't going to be deflected that easily.

She nodded and accepted the second card.

"Thanks again Jane."

"You're welcome. Good luck with your friend."

"Thank you," I said. And with that I was in the hall and on my way to the elevator.

Chapter 12

Jordan, Jordan, and Associates

Once I was back in the main lobby of the building I called Mark from my cell and got his voice mail. I left a message that I'd be there shortly and walked the Magnificent Mile towards the Loop.

Just before the Chicago River Bridge I turned right and cut through the walkway along the side of the Wrigley building. This brought me into the plaza behind the Sun Times. Vibrant yellow mums filled a circular garden. I love finding these little garden islands in the midst of the tall city buildings. This one had the added attraction of leading to one of the most interesting building corridors I've ever seen, right through the Sun Times Building. This little known public walkway has a glass wall that overlooks the Sun Times printing presses. I watched the giant rollers turn out a steady stream of papers as I walked quickly through the hallway above them. Exiting the Sun Times Building, I crossed Wabash Avenue and walked across one of the windiest places in the city, the IBM Plaza. On the worst of the wind days there are actually poles screwed into the cement plaza holding guide ropes to keep the lighter pedestrians earth bound. Then walking across the bridge, I was on the corner of Wabash and Wacker. Mark's office is on this corner, at the northeast edge of the Loop, in the old Jewelers' Building.

The building gets its name from its early days as the home of many of the city's wholesale jewelry dealers. Originally, the jewelers could actually drive their cars into the building from lower Wacker. An elevator carried them in their cars to their floor. Each floor had a parking area in its core and offices on the perimeter of the building, some with magnificent views of the Chicago River. The idea was to provide a safety feature for the jewelers traveling with precious gem stones. This interior parking lot has long since been turned into office space. The city's jewel dealers left the building but the name remains.

Another unusual feature of the building is a circular tower on the top two floors, reached by a separate brass elevator. I've heard stories that Al Capone had his headquarters on these floors during Prohibition. They are now home to the law firm of Jordan, Jordan, and Associates.

Mark and his brother, Robert, started their firm in 1982. It grew quickly and now has twenty-five lawyers. They're a boutique by Chicago standards but exactly as large as they want to be. Mark specializes in commercial real estate and Robert in commercial litigation. Each of them has developed a department of lawyers in his own specialty, and there are a few lawyers practicing corporate law and estate planning.

I rode the brass elevator up to the twentieth floor and entered the central reception area. Marcia greeted me and said Mark was expecting me. He was in the conference room with clients and had left word that I should make myself comfortable in his office. He'd meet me as soon as his meeting ended. Great, that would give me time to think about my own meetings and make a few notes.

As I settled into the sofa and pulled out my notebook, Robert walked by. He was taller and thinner than Mark, but with the same dark hair and blue eyes. He glanced into the office. He gave me a surprised smile, then came in and gave me a hug hello.

"Karen, how good to see you!"

"Good to see you too, Bob."

"Hey, I'm so sorry about your friend Alice. Mark told me, of course. Frank's a good lawyer. He'll have her out of there in no time."

"Thanks Bob, I hope so. Alice's been in jail for two days now. But she should have been out on bail this morning. I've been asking around, trying to see who else might have had a motive."

"Any luck?"

"Well, I've just started asking questions. So far, I think something was going on between George's wife and a fellow named David Canter. How that fits in with this I don't know yet."

"Who've you talked to?"

"Well, George's neighbor, Polly. I don't know if you know her?"

"No, don't think we've met. What's her last name?"

"Andrews."

"Polly Andrews? As in Andrews Public Relations?"

"Right, that's her firm. Have you worked with her?

"Yes, she represents one of my client's companies. You don't think she's involved in George's murder do you?"

"No, no. I just wanted to see what I could learn about George's wife, Darlene, and his son, Max. Turns out, Polly has a pretty good view of George and Darlene's place from her window. She apparently pays pretty close attention to who's coming and going over there. She told me David's been visiting Darlene regularly while George was out. I also spoke to David. He tells me he and Darlene are 'just friends'."

"So you think they're still lovers and that they killed George for his money?"

"Well, that's a pretty big jump from the fact that Darlene and David still see each other. Could be they're just friends as he says, but then again—"

"Right. Who else did you talk to today?"

"I met with Richard Fox, George's old partner."

"Richard Fox—that name is so familiar. What kind of business is he in?"

"Well, from the looks of his office I'd say he's just about retired. But he practiced law with George. They set up their firm together."

Suddenly Bob's eyes lit up with recognition. "Oh, it's coming back to me—it was a long time ago—he was one of the lawyers in Graylord."

"You mean trying the case for the feds? I don't think he was ever a prosecutor."

"No, I mean he was one of the lawyers they said was paying off judges to fix criminal cases."

"Oh no," I gasped and shook my head. "I don't think so—he did bankruptcy law."

"No, no, I remember this. They never made the case against him stick, but he was in the papers for weeks. The scuttlebutt was that the feds were sure he was crooked. They had a lot of evidence, but they lacked a smoking gun and in the end his lawyer got him off at trial."

"Are you sure you are thinking of the right guy—Richard Fox?"

"I'm sure. I know it was twenty years ago, but I remember—I hadn't been practicing very long and that whole investigation made a big impression on me. I didn't know that kind of corruption existed and I followed the cases every day— reading the papers and learning what I could from the talk at the Bar Association and around the courts. As I remember it, he kept his license because he was acquitted. He stopped practicing criminal law and just focused on his bankruptcy practice."

"Really? Do you remember what year that was?"

"I think it was in the early 80's—something like that."

"Hmm, funny Alice hadn't mentioned anything like that to me," I said.

"Well, that was ancient history. I don't see how it could be relevant to George's murder," Bob said.

"Well, you never know. I want to learn more about it anyway. I remember Graylord was well covered in the press. And there should be court records."

"Really, I don't know how that could be connected to his partner's murder some twenty years later," Bob said.

"Maybe it's not. But it's strange enough that I want to follow up on it," I said.

"Counselor, think you can still find your way to the court house?" he asked kidding me about my career change.

"Yes, I think I'll be able to do that," I said with a smile.

"Hey, what are you two chuckling about in here? Don't you know this is a law office?" Mark came into the room, beaming, and put his arm around my waist.

"Your brother was filling me in on some legal history that may help me with Alice. He was telling me that George's old partner, Richard Fox, was involved in the Graylord investigation. He was actually tried but they didn't convict him."

"Interesting, but how would that relate to George's murder?" Mark asked.

"Well, I don't know that it does, but it certainly is something out of the ordinary so I'll see what I can learn about it," I said.

"So, how was your meeting?" I asked Mark. Clearly he was in a good mood about something.

"You're looking at the new lawyer for the first multigenerational assisted living complex in Illinois."

"Hey, congratulations!" Bob said.

"Sounds great, but what is a multigenerational assisted living complex?" I asked.

"It's a way to integrate the generations—let the elderly interact with orphaned children, let the kids get the benefit of having adopted grandparents who want their company. We think this could be good for both the young and the old and save the state in care costs as well," Mark explained.

"Where will it be located?"

"We haven't settled on that yet. The developer is talking with two communities right now and we'll see which will be more supportive. But it'll probably be outside the central metro area."

The phone rang and Mark's secretary announced a call from Frank Bonafiglio. Mark took the call and put him on speaker.

"Mark, hi, it's Frank."

"Frank, hi, I've got you on speaker. Karen is here and my brother Robert."

"Hi Karen, Robert. I just tried calling you Karen, but didn't get through. So I thought I'd check in with Mark and give him the good news."

"You've gotten Alice out?" I asked.

"Yes, and she's home and very grateful to you. But we've got a lot of work to do. The State's Attorney seems hooked on the idea that this is a domestic killing—no signs of robbery, the body was found on her property, motive he figures as revenge for the divorce. Have you found any ammunition for me to shoot down his theory?"

"Nothing concrete yet, but I may be on to something. Seems Darlene has been seeing her old boyfriend, David Canter, on the sly. Could be they were in this together to get George's money and then get him out of the way," I said.

"Could be," Frank said.

"And I met with George's old partner, Richard Fox."

"Of Graylord fame?" Frank asked.

"Does everybody know this but me?" I asked.

"Well, it's pretty old stuff, but as trial lawyers, we all paid a lot of attention to that investigation, as you can imagine. If all your hard work meant nothing in the face of corrupt judges, you'd pay attention too," Frank said.

"Yes, I suppose. Anyway, Fox didn't have much to tell me. Graylord didn't come up, that's for sure. He operates out of an office in the Hancock, but there were no signs of any active business being conducted. I figure he's semi-retired and his office is just a place for him to go during the day. I'll read his Graylord case file, but I don't see where he has any current connection to George," I said.

"Well, remember, it's still up to the State's Attorney to make the case against Alice. And so far, it's all circumstantial evidence," Frank said.

"But the fact is that George was found on her property and that her finger prints are on the fire iron that killed him," Mark said.

"That's a lot of circumstantial evidence against her, especially given the ugly divorce and the fact that George left her," I said.

"True. So let's open up some room for doubt. We need to develop some other scenarios for George's murder. And it sounds like you're making progress on that, Karen," Frank said.

"Some," I answered. "When do you think the trial will be?" I asked Frank.

"Probably in about six weeks. We'll have some motion procedures to go through and the Court will have to schedule the case. Those things will take time, but the State's Attorney will press for an early trial," Frank said.

"The funeral services are this Thursday," I said. "I plan to go and I'll let Alice know about it. I don't think she'll want to go. But, then again, she may. You know, she was married to him for twenty-two years."

"That's true. But it would be awkward for her to be there, being the main suspect in his murder," Mark said, nodding. "I don't think she should go."

"I wouldn't recommend it either, but it's up to her. Well, I'm going to have to hang up now. I want to pack up and head back home tonight," Frank said.

"Oh, of course. Thanks, Frank. Drive carefully. You know, Highway 20 has the highest accident rate in the state. It's all hills and twisty two lanes with lots of trucks," I said.

"I'll be careful," Frank said. "Let's touch base in a couple days and let me know what you've come up with."

"Will do," I said.

"Thanks Frank. I really appreciate your handling this case for us. I know it's a pain driving all the way out there," Mark said.

"Not at all. It gives me time to think while I'm driving. I'll be in touch." And with that, Frank rang off.

Robert headed back to his office and Mark and I called it a day and headed to his place.

We spent the evening talking to Alice, then ordering in dinner from Connie's, our favorite Chicago pizza place. We tucked in early and fell asleep in the comfort of each other's arms.

Chapter 13

Court Files and Other Ancient History

We woke to Tuesday morning's autumn sunrise over Lake Michigan. Orange light gleamed on the water and spray from the waves glistened brightly as they crashed against the breakwater. Staying in bed was tempting, but we both had a full day ahead and we'd agreed we were jogging this morning. So somewhat reluctantly, we both rolled out of bed and pulled jogging clothes over our sleepy selves. Half awake, we headed for the path along the lakefront. We walked the two blocks to the park as our warm up and then Mark blew me a kiss and took off doing wind sprints. I watched him disappear ahead of me in the tunnel crossing Lakeshore Drive. I wanted to ease into my run and think this morning. As I emerged from the tunnel onto the path along the beach, the light glistening on the water filled my eyes. I broke into an easy jog and made my way out to the spiral point of the Oak Street Beach breakwater. A few gulls moved through the crisp morning air. Other joggers and walkers put in their miles, nodding as they went by.

I'd put in my five miles and was already out of the shower when Mark returned. He'd jogged his usual ten miles and was flushed with the exertion. He did his fifteen minute stretch routine while I crunched cereal at the counter and watched him. His culinary passion's propensity to add pounds was kept in check by his vigorous morning runs. He looked thirty-five instead of forty-five.

"So, what's your plan for the day?" Mark asked, his breathing back to its normal pace.

"Federal Court Building first. I want to see what I can learn about the Fox trial."

"Well, records that old are probably in storage. You'll have to order them up and it may take a while. You could always do some research at the newspapers.   And I'll set you up with an office and computer connection if you want to do some research at our offices."

"Thanks, I'll take you up on that. It'll be good to have a place to work from and take calls while I'm working on this."

"And I like the idea of being able to walk down the hall to see you—" he said.

"Definitely one of the advantages of my being in the city," I said and smiled. "Of course, if we were both in the country, then it would be an advantage of the country now wouldn't it?"

We had a long standing debate about the relative merits of city life versus country life. Neither of us had succeeded in converting the other thus far. But the combination of the two worlds seemed to work pretty well.

I put my cereal bowl in the dishwasher and headed to the bedroom to dress.

Mark hit the shower and was just getting out when I went to kiss him goodbye. He looked so good in his towel I hated to leave, but duty called. Alice's freedom might very well depend on my work. I wasn't counting on the State's Attorney or the Galena sheriff's detectives to do much digging. They thought they had the case solved already. And Frank needed a theory to work with if he was going to get Alice acquitted.

When I talked to Alice last night she was relieved to be home, but worried about her trial. I asked her what she knew about Rich Fox's Graylord trial. It turns out that that trial had happened several years before she met George. The whole subject had been taboo. They never talked about it. And if someone at a party or a dinner brought it up, the subject was quickly changed. She had assumed it was out of respect for Rich that George refused to talk about it, but she shed little light on the subject for me. Maybe I was wasting my time with ancient history that had nothing to do with George's murder. But I figured the only way I could know that for sure was to learn what I could about the case.

The Federal Court Clerk's office was just opening as I made my way through the glass and steel government doors. The clerk at the counter directed me to a small office down the hall where I filled out a file request form and another clerk informed me it would take forty-eight hours to retrieve the file. However, he said if I just need to read the transcript of the trial, that is on microfiche and he could call it up for me right away. I jumped at the offer and was directed to a bank of computer like terminals. I took a seat on the stool in front of the first terminal and waited for the film to be delivered to me. Three other seats were occupied by young lawyers, who were probably doing the legwork for lawyers my age.   The film was brought to me and, as I read on, it became apparent that something had drastically changed in the prosecutor's case about midway through the trial. They had asked for a recess and then a conference with the judge in his chambers. The conference was off the record, but when they returned the judge instructed the jury that the prosecutors would not be calling George Almonte to testify as originally promised. No more was said about this by either the prosecutor or the judge. I scrolled back to the opening statements and reread the prosecutor's statement: "We will offer evidence from Mr. Fox's own partner, George Almonte, of a conversation he personally heard between Mr. Fox and Judge Zenera."

Wow! So George was going to testify against Richard Fox. Then for some reason he changed his mind. But Richard and George had continued to work together for years after this. That didn't seem to make sense. You'd think Fox would want to be as far from George as possible. Unless he saw George's refusal as being instrumental in getting him acquitted. And George, for his part, if he thought Richard was bribing judges, why would he want to remain partners? Maybe George was blackmailing Richard, or maybe George was involved in the bribery himself. The prosecutors could have called George even if he had changed his story. If George had given them a sworn statement before trial, they could have impeached him with his own statement.   But the prosecution must have figured that didn't give them anything except confusion and doubt in the minds of the jurors. Or maybe they hadn't gotten a sworn statement from George. Maybe they'd gone on his word. That's pretty common practice. In any event, they'd elected to go with the other circumstantial evidence and in the end failed to convince the jury. They had Judge Zenera's clerk testify to numerous visits by Richard to the Judge. Richard and the Judge both testified they were merely friends. The prosecutors introduced bank account records showing monthly two thousand dollar withdrawals from Rich's account and similar deposits to the Judge's. Rich said this was his monthly personal spending money.

The Judge said his deposits were transfers from other accounts and were used to pay personal expenses. In the end, the prosecutors failed to convince the jury of Richard's involvement beyond a reasonable doubt.

I wondered if George had been holding this change in his story over Richard all these years? Maybe that was at the root of their later estrangement. I made notes of the names of the other witnesses and the prosecutor and defense attorney in the case. The attorneys might still be practicing and, even if they weren't, they'd surely remember this case. My best chance of finding them would probably be through the Illinois Attorney Registration and Disciplinary Commission. After making my notes, I thanked the clerk and said I'd be back Thursday morning to look at the original court file.

I traced my steps back along the worn gray carpeting to the bank of steel elevators. A young man in a pinstriped suit was waiting at the elevator bank and we rode in elevator silence down the twenty floors to the Dirksen Building's main floor. The bright sun made me squint as I gazed across the crowded plaza. Tuesday is Market Day. The vendors and their brightly colored flowers, fruits and vegetables stood in stark relief to the dreary record offices. This was the last of the season's Farmers' Markets and was in full noon hour swing. Office workers filled their arms with plastic bags of ripe tomatoes, grapes, apples and fall flowers. Others carried gourds or ate homemade cookies and drank cider. The lunch crowd filled the too few benches. People gathered around the orange steel legs of the giant Calder sculpture talking. Other folks were eating their lunches and basking in the rays of sunshine and crisp fall air.

I bought an apple and a bag of nuts and walked east the three blocks to the Art Institute. The gardens along the south side of the Art Institute are one of my favorite places to sit and think. There is a canopy of carefully trimmed trees, their arching branches forming a lacy umbrella over the bench lined walkways. This time of year the leaves are golden and light shines through them like an intricate stained glass window. I chose a seat near the large sculpture at the eastern edge of the garden, which gave me a view back across this light dappled refuge. Michigan Avenue and its crush of people and cars seemed a world away from this quiet landscaped spot. Maybe it was the juxtaposition of the crowd to this garden that added to its charm. I ate my lunch in this lovely hideaway and then decided to rejoin the world with a call to Frank.

I found my cell phone in the bottom of my purse and dialed Frank's direct number. He was in his office and said he was anxious to hear what I'd learned.

"I spent the morning looking at microfiche of the court transcript of Richard Fox's trial. Seems awfully long ago to be connected to George's death, but I did find that George was supposed to testify against Richard. He apparently changed his story during the trial, and was never called as a witness. It looks like that change was instrumental in Richard's acquittal."

"Interesting. Any record of what his testimony would have been?"

"No, since George didn't testify the evidence never was introduced, except for an early reference by the prosecutor saying George would testify about a conversation he had heard between Richard and Judge Zenera. What ever he'd been saying to the prosecutors before trial didn't become a part of the court transcript. Don't think there'll be anything about that in the court file either. So, I was thinking I'd try to track down the prosecutor. I don't think George's defense attorney will want to talk to me. And client privilege would prevent him from telling me much in any event."

"That's probably right. I think the prosecutor is your best bet, if he's still around."

"The prosecutor's name in the court transcript was Martin Thomas. Does that name mean anything to you?"

"No, but here, let me check my Sullivan's and I'll see if he's still listed." The speaker phone picked up the rustle of turning pages. Then Frank said, "Thomas, Martin, born 1935, admitted to the bar in 1959. Office is listed at 178 West Washington. That would be across from the Daley Center. Looks like you'll have to follow up, but at least you know he was still kicking last year when the info for this book was gathered."

"Great. Thanks, Frank. Have you heard anything from the State's Attorney in Galena or the Coroner's office?" I asked.

Murder in Galena

"I have a call in to the Coroner. The State's Attorney has asked for a meeting with me this Friday. When will you be going back home?"

"Well, I want to be here for the services on Thursday. Depending on what comes up, I may go home on Friday as well."

"Have you talked to the widow Almonte yet?" Frank asked.

"Not yet. I may pay her a visit this afternoon."

"Let me know what you think after you meet with her."

"Will do. Talk to you later then," I said.

"Bye. And be careful out there."

So, Frank is meeting with the State's Attorney on Friday. That gives me two and a half days to come up with some alternative scenarios that Frank can suggest to the State's Attorney at their meeting.

I decided to go to Darlene's unannounced and see if she would talk to me.

69

Chapter
14

Darlene's

I left the relative peace of the garden and stood along the Michigan Avenue curb with my arm out. A yellow cab screeched to a stop and I climbed in. Ten minutes and a jerky cab ride later I was on Astor Street standing in front of the three story brownstone in which Darlene and George had made their home. I walked through the black wrought iron gate and rang the bell on the side of the carved door. Darlene answered in a static filled voice. I told her I was an old friend and country neighbor of George's and had come to pay my condolences. There was a pause and, surprisingly, the buzzer sounded. I opened the door and went up the stairs. Darlene's voice called to me saying, "Up here."

I knew my way through the house. I'd been there many times before when George and Alice were married. I found Darlene sitting on the green sofa by the fireplace in the den.

"Darlene, I'm so sorry for your loss," I said.

"Thank you. George has mentioned you many times in telling me about his life in the country. You were good friends with Alice weren't you?"

"Yes, I was and I still am."

"Oh. And what brings you here?"

"As a friend of Alice and George's I want to make sure the right person is held accountable for his murder. And right now, I think the police are on the wrong track."

She looked at me with disdain. "I think they're on exactly the right track. Alice has hated me and George ever since the divorce."

"That's not true," I said. "She still cared very much for George." I let Darlene's statement about Alice's feelings for her stand. What could I say? Alice did hate Darlene.

"Tell me about your relationship with David Canter."

"I don't have a relationship with him," she said. She rose and backed away from me. "What is this? Are you accusing me?" she asked and glared at me.

"I am not accusing you of anything. I only asked about David Canter. He was seen visiting here over the past few months."

"So, she was spying on me and George?"

"Who?"

"Alice, of course. Who else would be so obsessed?"

"No, it wasn't Alice who saw Canter coming here. Why don't you just tell me about your relationship with him if there's nothing to hide?"

"Because I don't think I like your tone. And it's none of your or anyone else's business. Maybe you should just leave," Darlene said.

"Look, you're going to have to answer these questions for the police. And if they don't ask them, Alice's lawyer will ask them, under oath. So you might as well practice your answers on me. Otherwise, I suppose I'll have to testify that you got very upset when I told you David Canter had been seen coming and going while George was out. Doesn't sound very good that way now does it?"

"Oh forget it. That isn't going anywhere. David is just a friend. I've been lonely. I don't see anyone but George since we got married. I quit work. And he goes out and rides his horses and chums around with all those horse people out there. I hate those damn horses. They could kill you without even knowing it."

"So you called your old friend, David, to keep you company."

"Just someone to talk to—"

"Why did you do it when George was out?"

"Why do you think?" she said looking at me. Then quickly added, "No, I don't mean that—I mean because George was insanely jealous. He was afraid I'd miss David for other reasons. You know what I mean? George was forty years older than me and so maybe he wasn't so secure about keeping me from looking at other guys, if you know what I mean."

"Did he have reason to be jealous?"

"Hey, I have everything I want: a nice house, money like I never dreamed. So what if he isn't—wasn't—the biggest stud around."

"And why David then?"

"I told you, he was just for company, someone my age to talk to."

"Uh huh." I nodded, but I wasn't buying it.

"What about Max? How did George and Max get along?"

"Oh—Max is one angry, mixed up kid."

"Why do you say that?"

"Cause he would call up George and yell and scream at him one day and then call back and ask for money the next. He never let up."

"I heard he was in a rehab program in California."

"Yah. You wouldn't believe it—Max had been asking George for three hundred thousand dollars for a down payment on a new house. Guy doesn't work, just calls up his old man and harasses money out of him. Well, George figures his kid is going to get the money someday anyway and, if Max doesn't get off the drugs, he's going to lose everything he gets. So, George made a deal with Max. If Max stays in a rehab program for six months, George will give him the three hundred thousand. Max whined, but the next day he checked himself into a program."

"How did George know Max was in the program?"

"The director guy called George. Said Max would only be allowed one call a week and personal visits once a week. But George could call and talk to the director guy anytime he wanted."

"So how long has Max been in the program?"

"Well, it's about six weeks now I think."

"Have you told him about his father?"

"Yah, I called the place and told the director. Thought Max should be back here for the funeral."

"How is Max doing?"

"He's all right. The director said Max was sick last week, some flu bug, but he's better and he's coming here tomorrow."

"Is he staying here?"

"No way! Max stays at the Ritz. Annoyed the hell out of George when Max did that. Waste of money, George would say. But Max wanted the best all the time. Didn't care about the cost—he never had to work for a dime in his life. Anyway, he hated me. So he wouldn't be staying here anyway."

"He hated you? Why?"

" 'Cause I was cutting into his bucks. He wanted George's money all to himself."

"And as the widow you get half of everything George had, is that right?"

"Hah! Hardly! It's lots more complex than that. There are trusts that give stock and stuff to Max, one for charity, and one for me. There's not much that's not in one of those trusts. But I'll be all right. George took care of me so I won't have to go back to the gym any time soon. And I keep this place too," she said, looking around at the high ceilings, chandeliers and fireplace. The townhouse had to be worth at least five million dollars itself.

"So you and Max don't talk?"

"No, he did enough yelling at his father that I didn't want to have anything to do with the brat. Sooner he's back in California the better as far as I'm concerned. Don't see that he'll bring anything but trouble with him. Spoiled, spoiled, spoiled." This from the exercise instructor who had just inherited a five million dollar home and probably another thirty million to go along with it.

"Well, I guess I'll have a chance to meet him after the funeral on Thursday," I said, taking the opportunity to invite myself.

"Yah, sure, come over after the funeral. He'll probably come here, just to tell me that this should be his house—but I don't see how I can stop him from coming—and it's just one afternoon—then he's out of my life."

"Well, I won't take any more of your time Darlene. Thanks for talking to me."

"No sweat. But you're wasting your time trying to get Alice off the hook. She was just nuts, you know—couldn't stand the fact that George had left her and that she'd lost this place. She did it—I just know it."

"Well Darlene, I don't think she did. But thank you for seeing me and I'll see you on Thursday."

"Yah, Thursday."

"I'll see myself out," I said and left her sitting in front of the fireplace in her mansion.

As I walked down the stairs, it struck me how unemotional Darlene was about George's death. Maybe she was still in shock. Maybe she just didn't really care about him. I didn't know which it was, but I needed to find out.

The afternoon light cast long shadows on the sidewalk as I exited Darlene's home. I figured it was time to head back to Mark's office, check messages, and give Alice a call.

I walked down the narrow sidewalk on State Street, crowded with its usual mix of wealthy professionals, poverty line workers, and street people. As I came to the corner of State and Chicago, a man in a gray coat with a hat pulled low over his face came running around the corner straight into me. The force of his forward momentum knocked me off my feet and sent me sprawling onto the sidewalk. I tried to brace myself for the fall and felt a sharp pain in my left shoulder as I hit the ground. The guy didn't stop and, by the time I picked myself up, he was long gone in the crowd. Two people stopped to ask if I was all right, but more just looked and walked on.

I didn't see anyone chasing this fellow. At least I assumed it was a man from the force of the blow and the trench coat and hat he'd been wearing. My shoulder ached, but I could move my hand and arm, so I figured nothing was broken. I brushed off my coat, assured the woman and gentleman who were standing next to me that I was all right, and continued on my way to Mark's office. A few minutes later my cell phone rang. I barely heard the ringing above the sounds of city traffic. I fished the phone from my purse, flipped it open, and pressed the phone to my right ear. I held my other hand over my left ear in an effort to block out the ambient sounds and said, "Hello."

"I could have shot you. This is your only warning. Stop meddling." The voice was deep and distorted. Someone was trying to disguise their voice by talking below their normal range and slowing their speech pattern. I thought it was a man, but it could have been a woman talking in a lower octave. Tying the low voice with the force of the blow, I was betting on a man. Well, my inquiries were certainly making someone nervous! The question was, "Who?" Darlene had seemed quite calm. A little less upset than I imagined the average widow would be, but not threatened by my presence. Rich Fox didn't look like the type to knock me over on the street. Of course, he could have hired someone to do that for him. That would seem more his style. Knocking me down could be something David Canter would do, more brawn than brain.

I found myself in front of Mark's office building, stepped into the pie shaped space of the revolving glass door, and pushed ahead.

Chapter 15

Mark's office

The receptionist at Mark's office gave me a strange look as I walked in. "Hello Ms. Prince. Mark asked me to show you to your office when you got here. It's right this way. Can I help you with your coat?" she asked as she rose and stepped around the crescent desk.

As I turned my back to her to let her take my coat, I saw my reflection in the reception room mirror. There was dirt all along the left side of my coat and my mascara had run, forming dark marks along my right cheek. I vaguely remembered tears welling in my eyes as I lay on the sidewalk, which I had quickly brushed away. They'd left a black trail in their path.

"Thank you. I think I'll stop in the ladies room for just a minute," I said and excused myself. In the strong fluorescent light I looked even worse than I had in the diffused light of the reception area. There was a long scrape on the left side of my face where I'd hit the sidewalk. Lovely. I washed off the dirt with little globs of soap from the soap dispenser and used wet paper towels to remove the black mascara streaks from my cheek. I gave my hair a quick comb through and finger fluff and returned to the receptionist.

"Much better," I said and smiled, willing her not to inquire any further. I knew I'd be the topic of conversation in the coffee room, but I didn't want to get into explanations now.

The young receptionist led me down the hall to a small interior office with a desk, phone, and computer terminal. "Your phone extension is 4557, Ms. Prince. If you need anything just call me. Mr. Jordan's office is right down the hall to your left."

"Thank you. Could you tell Mark I'm here and ask him to stop by when he has a chance?"

"Certainly, Ms. Prince." And with that the still wide eyed young woman left me in my new office.

I fired up the computer and entered notes from my day's interviews. David Canter seemed my strongest bet. He was seeing the now rich widow. I didn't yet have a feeling for whether or not Darlene was involved.

I went to the website for Beachfront and got the name and number of the director. I knew I'd have to talk to the top person there if I was going to learn anything at all about Max. Anyone else on staff would just follow procedure and tell me that all patient information was private, as well it should be. I hoped to impress the director enough to agree to meet with me. I could fly out on Friday and meet him on Saturday. Before I called, I did a Google search and did some background reading on the Beachfront. Founded in 1975 by Doctor Charles Wilson, the clinic specializes in alcohol and drug rehabilitation of the rich and famous, including corporate executives, actors and actresses, and the scions of the world's wealthiest families. The clients are clearly accustomed to luxury and price is not a deciding factor. All rooms are private suites or stand alone cabins. The facility occupies two hundred acres of prime California coast land. From the pictures, it looks more like a resort than an institution. It's a sort of spa, offering psychiatric help, as well as classes on yoga, nutrition and stress management. The facility has a gourmet restaurant, tennis and golf facilities, and a movie theater. Rates begin at twenty-five hundred dollars per day. Guess that will keep out the riff raff.

I considered approaching Doctor Wilson as a TV journalist, but figured publicity was not what he sought, it was privacy. Then I thought of pretending to be a government inspector, but didn't know enough about his industry to bluff my way through that on the phone. Well, what did I have to lose? I picked up the phone and dialed the Beachfront's number. A pleasantly voiced woman answered and asked how she could direct my call. I asked for Doctor Wilson and was connected to his secretary.

Doctor Wilson, it seemed, was with a patient and then scheduled to give a lecture to the residents. After some discussion, I was able to schedule an appointment to meet with Doctor Wilson and tour the facility. Seems my Aunt Rose is in need of an extended stay at just such a facility. But she hates to travel and I promised to take a look at it before she considered making the trip. Aunt Rose is having difficulty adjusting to the responsibilities of being a wealthy widow. She needed to get away for at least a month.

That settled, I tried checking in with Alice at her home. No answer. I left a message and dialed her cell phone. She picked up on the second ring and sounded out of breath. "Hey Allie, it's me. How are you holding up?"

"I'm sweaty and covered in mud! I've been working off my frustrations by digging up the hostas from the front garden and putting them in along the side of the shed. How's it going in the city? Learn anything to help save me yet?" This bravura was Alice's style, but I knew she was scared and didn't want to show it.

"Well, I seem to be touching a nerve with someone. I got a call telling me to stay out of this. A guy knocked me down on the sidewalk, to let me know he was here and could get to me I guess."

"Be careful Karen! Who do you think you've set off?"

"Well, I've talked to all my main suspects here: Canter, Fox, and the delightful Darlene."

"What did she have to say?"

"Basically, she thinks you did it and that I'm wasting my time."

"The slut. I'd say she and her boyfriend did it and would like to let me hang for it. What did I ever do to her? First she takes my husband, then she's living in my house, and now she wants to put me in prison!"

"Hey, we don't know that she did it. Wild accusations aren't going to do us any good. We need some concrete evidence."

"Do we have any—that doesn't incriminate me, I mean?"

"We have Polly saying that David Canter is a regular visitor of the sweet Darlene. Seems he kept her company while George was out riding his horse."

"Yes, and I'll bet she was riding too."

"We don't know that, but it's possible. Oh, and I just learned that George was supposed to testify against Richard Fox at Fox's bribery trial."

"Really? I didn't know that! Like I said, that was before we were married and George never talked about it. I only learned about Fox's trial when I came across some old files in a box at home. When I asked George about it, he said it was a long time ago. He said that early in their law careers, there'd been an older criminal lawyer who officed on the same floor as they did. The lawyer asked Richard to help him with a few cases and led Richard down a path he shouldn't have taken. George said it had nothing to do with him."

"Did Richard's wife ever talk about the Graylord trial?"

"No, never—and neither did I. It would have seemed awfully rude to bring it up to either of them. I knew it was a painful subject, so I avoided it. It was so long ago, I don't see what it can have to do with George's death anyway."

"Well, maybe it doesn't have anything to do with it. I just want to tie up the loose end of why George and Richard parted ways."

"Yes, I guess that makes sense."

"Have you heard from Max?" I asked.

"He called and said he was coming in for the funeral. I told him I'd decided not to go. It would just be too much—and who'd I be going there for? It'll just be Darlene and Max and George's business associates. I've been out of his life for two years now, so I guess I'll stay out of his funeral too."

"Probably a wise decision—you don't need a lot of people staring at you. And I wouldn't put it past Darlene or David to make a scene––especially if they're trying to sway public opinion against you."

"I know—it's all just so unreal. It's—hard."

"I wish I was there with you—and that I could do more for you."

"You're doing so much Karen. And I appreciate it."

"You'd do the same for me," I said. There was a pause as we both collected ourselves. Then I went on, "I'm going to go to the funeral. I want to see if I can talk to Max."

"Max? Max was in California. I don't see how he could have killed George from there."

"Well, I don't either right now, but since he was fighting with George, and since he's inheriting a fortune, I'd say he has a pretty strong motive."

"Well, tell him you're helping me and maybe he'll talk to you."

"Thanks, I'll use that as my intro to him. How are things going at the gallery while you're away?"

"Everything sounds like it's going along all right. Between the phone and the computer it's pretty easy to stay in touch. And Brenda can handle everything. Sales have actually been better than usual."

"Good, I'm glad that part of your life isn't being ruined by this."

"Yes, thank God."

"Well, I'd better go. I'll talk to you soon. Is Donald still there?"

"No, he headed back to the city. He had meetings he had to make, but he's coming back out here this weekend."

"Good, better for you to have company. I'm flying to California Friday. I have an appointment with the head of the Beachfront."

"And he's meeting with you about Max?"

"Well, he thinks he's meeting with me about my Aunt Rose."

"What Aunt Rose?"

"The one I made up yesterday so he'd meet with me."

"I see—well, be careful."

"You too. I'm sending Louise to check in on you, so don't be frightened if you hear someone knocking on your door tonight."

"You don't have to do that, I'm fine."

"Well, it'll make me feel better, so just humor me kiddo. And anyway, she'd love to see you. She thinks of you as a member of our extended family you know."

"Love you."

"Love you too. Bye."

So, Alice is all right, Mark is working, and I'm set to go to California on Friday. Thursday I'll meet Max and go to Darlene's in the afternoon. That leaves me Wednesday to find and talk to the prosecutor, Martin Thomas, about the Fox case. As I began another Google search to see what background I could unearth, my Prince Charming filled the frame of my doorway.

"Hey, how're you doing there?"

"Well, its been a long day, I'd say. You were right this morning. Fox's court files are in storage, but I did get to look at the microfiche. There was definitely something strange going on with that case. George was going to testify against Fox, but the prosecutor pulled him as a witness at the last minute. George must have changed his story. I'm going to try to talk to the prosecutor tomorrow and see what he'll tell me. I'm thinking I'll go to his office and see if I can't talk my way into seeing him. And, the big news of the day—someone actually ran into me and then called me on my cell phone to try to scare me off the case."

"What! When did this happen? What did they say?"

"Happened on State and Chicago and whoever it was didn't say much—basically, just told me to stay out of this."

"I'm sure he asked you nicely—"

"Well, he said he could have shot me and to stop meddling."

"Whoa! I think it's time you called that Detective Cavanaugh and told him what's going on here."

"Maybe—but it seems to me he has his mind made up about Alice. I'd rather have some concrete evidence to give him before I call him."

"And I'd rather you call him and he take the heat from this anonymous caller."

"I don't even know who I'm getting upset. Darlene, David, Rich Fox—could be any one of them, or someone I haven't even come across yet."

"Well, whoever it is, they're close enough to know you're digging around in this."

"That's true. Well, tomorrow I'll talk with Martin Thomas, the prosecutor in the Fox case and see what he'll tell me about George and Rich. Thursday I'll talk to Max and Friday I'm flying to LA. I want to check out this place where Max has been staying and talk to the head of the facility there. Frank has a meeting with the State's Attorney this Friday and I'd like to give him as much info as possible before then."

"How about a quiet night at home tonight?"

"That sounds perfect."

"Good, let's head out now."

"Ready."

Chapter 16

Home for the Night

Lying on the wide leather lounge, Mark kissed my neck and pulled me closer to him. I put my champagne glass on the table and then took his glass from his hand and put it next to mine. Quiet time together is a rare luxury for us and I intended to enjoy every minute of it. This magic moment was interrupted by the insistent ringing of Mark's phone.

"Telemarketer," he said. "Let it ring."

But something set my senses on alert as the caller ID announced Louise was calling. I looked at Mark and left his warm embrace for the chilling ring of the phone.

"Louise, what's the matter?" I asked, knowing she wouldn't call unless there was some problem.

"It's Alice—I called the ambulance—but she doesn't look good!"

"What do you mean? What's happened?"

"Well, I came over here to check on her like you said and she didn't answer the door. So, I looked all over the yard calling for her, but I couldn't find her. Then I went back up to the house and I knocked again. She still didn't answer, so I tried the door. It was unlocked and the lights were on like she was there and all. I got scared she'd fallen or something had happened to her—so I went in and started calling for her again. I saw the stairs and went up to look for her—and there she was on the bed—with an empty bottle of pills by her—I just screamed. I tried to get her awake, but I couldn't. I called 911 and they're on their way here. This house is bad luck. Been so since the first owner, and—"

"Louise, stay calm. Can you get Alice to sit up at all?"

"No, she only moans and tosses sort of. I can't get her up."

"Well, keep talking to her. I'm going to call Donald and I'll call you back."

"What's the matter?" Mark was asking as I tried to look up Donald's number in the phone book.

"It looks like Alice has taken some sort of pills and Louise just found her. The ambulance is on its way, but you know out there it's all volunteer—it'll take the ambulance twenty minutes to get to her place once they leave and another twenty to get her to the hospital after they get her in the ambulance." I went back to looking up Donald's number and said, "I have to call Donald and have him go out there—maybe I should go out there too—"

"Don't drive tonight. You can call the hospital and talk to the doctor and to Donald."

"Mark, I just don't think she would have taken pills—we just talked this afternoon—"

"Let Donald go out there. You're in no condition to drive out there tonight. You can decide what to do in the morning when you know more. It sounds like she's going to be out of it tonight anyway. Louise will stay with her until Donald gets there."

Mark took the phone from me and had the operator connect us to Donald. He was home and said he'd leave right away. We gave him directions to the Galena hospital and he said he'd call when he got there.

"I can't get over Alice trying to kill herself!" Mark said, shaking his head.

"I didn't get that at all from talking to her this afternoon. The divorce was hard, yes, but she seemed to be adjusted to that, finally. And—oh no—you know the sheriff is going to call this a homicide-suicide," I said, as the picture of Detective Cavanaugh closing the case filled my mind.

"And you don't think so?" Mark asked.

"Of course not!"

"Then what?" he asked. "Why would she have taken the pills?"

"Maybe the loneliness, maybe the pressure of being accused," I said, trying on these answers.

"Well, she'll need our support when she comes around," Mark said.

"I hope she's all right," I sighed.

"Well, Louise will go with her to the hospital and she'll call us from there. Does Alice have any family?" Mark asked.

"One sister, but they really don't talk much. Her sister lives in California. They seem to have very little in common and I don't think they've seen each other in years," I told him.

"This is getting more and more bizarre," Mark said and put his arm around my shoulder.

Chapter 17

Martin Thomas

I woke up groggy on Wednesday. We'd been up most of the night talking to Louise and to the hospital, getting updates on Alice. The doctors had pumped her stomach and they expected her to make a full recovery. But they said it was a very close call. Alice had been lucky that Louise arrived just when she did.

Donald had gotten to the hospital about midnight and he'd been allowed to see her. She didn't seem to have any recollection of taking the pills, which the doctors attributed to shock and the effects of the drugs on her system. Louise hadn't found a note, just the bottle of pills. It was Alice's prescription, but it was two years old. She must have gotten the prescription about the time of the divorce and just had the pills in the medicine cabinet.

I called Frank and he'd spoken with the State's Attorney. As I'd feared, the State's Attorney was of the opinion that this made his case for him. Frank quoted the State's Attorney for me, "Murder, in general, is a crime of passion. Alice killed her ex-husband for leaving her and then was driven to kill herself out of guilt and fear of prison." Sounded exactly like something the judge and jury would buy.

I debated whether to drive out to Galena to see Alice or to stay in Chicago and continue my inquiries. In the end I decided to stick to my original plan. Alice would have Donald and Louise with her and we could talk by phone. If I didn't look into the alternatives to Alice as the murderer, it didn't seem that anyone else was going to make the effort. The local papers and the State's Attorney had already decided the outcome before the trial date had been set.

I showered and dressed and kissed Mark goodbye early Wednesday. A brisk walk into the Loop would help clear the cobwebs and I hoped to find Martin Thomas in his office before he got engaged in his appointments for the day.

Michigan Avenue traffic was jammed, four lanes across, stop and go. I found myself walking faster than the groaning busses, as they stopped at every corner to gather more office workers for the waiting Loop buildings. The store windows were filled with the latest fall and winter styles and I studied the clothing lines for the season as I walked by them.

Crossing the Michigan Avenue Bridge is always a fascinating sight, if you take the time to look at the reflections of light on the water and the varied architecture of the buildings along the river's edge. A few restaurants have opened along the river to take advantage of the view. Lower Wacker is just visible. That's the underground maze of streets used by trucks making deliveries to the office buildings above. Besides the truckers, a few knowledgeable drivers use this lower roadway to avoid the snarl of traffic above ground. The Lower Wacker infrastructure has been rusting away for years. After twenty years of reports of imminent doom and a few pieces of falling concrete, the city has finally started the long and expensive process of rebuilding the metal support system for Wacker Drive.

I followed the River west to State Street and then turned south. Strains of Sinatra filled my head singing, "State Street that great street, that toddling town." Traffic, once banned in the seventies move to rejuvenate aging downtowns, had now been re-introduced on State Street to attract more shoppers. And it seemed to be working. I walked past the queen of State Street, Marshall Fields. This gray stone, nine story building covered a full city block, a veritable monument to shopping.

Washington Avenue was at the far end of Marshall Fields and I turned right to walk the two blocks west to what I hoped would still be Martin Thomas's office. The needle thin office building I sought was located directly across from the Daley Center, the home of the municipal and county courts for the city. Lawyers filled the surrounding buildings, including this one. Its uniqueness lay in the fact that it housed a religious temple on its street level, leaving a small entry area with two banks of elevators to serve the office tower.

I scanned the directory and was relieved to find Martin Thomas still listed. So far so good. I took the elevator to the twentieth floor. The hall was surprisingly long in comparison to the small footprint of the lobby. Room 2021 was at the far end of the hall, around a corner and on the interior.   Judging from the location, I figured Mr. Thomas's practice was probably a small solo office, handling a few criminal cases. The door was closed, but the name Martin Thomas, Attorney at Law, was stenciled on it. I tried the handle. The door was unlocked so I knew someone was already in the office.   I hoped it was Thomas and not just his secretary.   I opened the door and walked into a small, dingy waiting room. A glass partition between this small room and the main office appeared to be the receptionist's station. I peered through the glass but I didn't see anyone. I thought of waiting a few minutes, but found myself trying the door to the right of the receptionist's glass window, which obviously led to the main part of the office.   The handle turned easily.   I called out as I opened the door, "Hello. Mr. Thomas? Hello—"

No answer.   The receptionist's desk was just below the glass partition to my left.   To the right was a hallway with three doors opening off the hallway.   I peaked into the first doorway and saw a smallish office with a single desk and two chairs.   The drawers to the desk were pulled out and the contents of several manila legal files lay strewn across the desk top. Curiosity and my desire to talk to Martin Thomas propelled me forward.   I called out again and moved down the hall to the second door.   Someone had beaten me here.   A man whom I presumed to be Mr. Thomas lay face down at his desk and files were strewn across the floor.   The shock sent a quick spurt of adrenaline through my system, heightening my senses.

I heard a sound in the third room.   I froze for a second, torn between running out of there and finding out what was going on.   I thought of what the heroines in my favorite mystery novels would do in a situation like this, braced myself, then slid along the wall toward the third door.   The noise continued—file drawers being pulled out, slammed shut.   I reached into my purse and pulled out the gun Mark had given me this morning. I don't like carrying a gun, but Mark had insisted on it after that threatening phone call. Now I was glad I had it. I was a good shot. A high school boyfriend had taught me to shoot a 22 in the sand dunes along Lake Michigan. I've had my own gun ever since I was twenty-one.

The third door was closed. I kicked it open and jumped to the side of the hall.   A shot exploded into the hallway wall across from the door.   Then deadly silence.

"Come out with your hands up. Police," I yelled, in as firm a voice as I could muster. I wondered if I could get arrested for impersonating an officer in a situation like this. Probably, but I thought it was my best chance to intimidate whoever was in there and make them think they were outnumbered.

"Throw your gun out and come out with your hands up," I called out again.

There was a rustling sound and then another shot. I heard a door open and then sounds of footsteps. I steeled myself and sprang into the room with my gun braced with both arms in front of me as I'd watched on so many television shows. The back door to the office was wide open and the office was empty. I ran to the hall just in time to see a man in his sixties running down the hall. He turned back to see if I was following and I gasped. The man running down the hall was Richard Fox.

I went back to the office and used the receptionist's phone to call 911. Then I went to check on the man I presumed was Martin Thomas. There was a gash on the back of his head, but his pulse still felt strong. The files on his desk seemed to be DUI cases. I wanted to check the files in the office Fox had been in before the police and paramedics arrived and I moved quickly back to that room. This seemed to be more of a file room, with a desk in the corner. Cabinet drawers were partially opened and files looked askew. Fox was definitely looking for something in particular. One cabinet drawer was fully extended. I put on my gloves and walked over to the drawer. The cabinet was labeled 1978. But Thomas had been a federal prosecutor back then. Case files from that time should have been a part of the government's files. Maybe these were his personal notes from the cases he'd handled. Maybe—just then I heard the real police in the front of the office.

"I'm in here. Karen Prince. I'm the one who called you." I didn't want to take any chances on being mistaken for the suspect. "Back here," I called out again.

"Please come out here, Ms. Prince," I heard.

Guess the officers weren't taking any chances either. I made sure my gun was tucked in the bottom of my purse and walked to the front of the office. There's an injured man in here. I think he's Martin Thomas and it looks like he's been hit on the head.

I came into the entry space with my ID in my raised hand. The officer nodded for me to come closer and took the ID, which was my driver's license.

"Ms. Prince, is there anyone else in this office?"

"Not that I know of, Officer O'Neill," I said, picking up his name from the badge on his jacket.

"All right, show me where this injured man is."

O'Neill, his partner and I walked back down the small hall to the second office, where the man I presumed to be Martin Thomas lay sprawled over the desk. O'Neill took Thomas's pulse and radioed for a detective to come to the scene. The second officer walked through the rest of the office, checking the layout. The paramedics arrived while we were still in Thomas's office and moved him to a stretcher. As we watched from the sidelines, Officer O'Neill turned to me and asked, "Well then, tell me what you're doing here this morning. Looks like you're a long way from home."

"I came here to talk to Mr. Thomas."

"Are you a client of Mr. Thomas?"

"No, I'm not. I wanted to ask him about a case he handled as a US Attorney a number of years ago."

"Did you have an appointment with him?"

"No, I just came in early, hoping to catch him before his morning appointments."

"And what did you do when you arrived?"

"I called out and when no one answered, I poked my head in the doorway by the receptionist's station and called for him. There wasn't any answer but the lights were on and all the doors had been unlocked, so I went in and took a look to see if I could find him."

"Do you usually walk into offices uninvited?"

"No, of course not, but it was really important that I find Mr. Thomas today and I guess that's what made me decide to look for him in the office when he didn't answer."

"And what did you do when you found him?"

"I checked his pulse and then I heard a noise from the next office."

"What kind of noise?"

"Like someone opening drawers and tossing files around."

"And what did you do then?"

"I figured it might be the person who had knocked out Mr. Thomas, so I crept along the hallway wall and I must have made a noise, because the next thing I knew there was a gun shot fired through the doorway." Something kept me from giving him the exact details—probably self preservation.

"And why didn't you just run out of here?"

"I don't know—I just wanted to try to catch the person who'd done this."

"Playing cop huh? Good way to get yourself killed, Ms. Prince."

I continued, "There was another shot and I heard the back door open, so figured whoever it was had left. I ran into the room and looked out into the hall. I saw a man run down the hall and go into the stairwell."

"Could you identify this man?"

"He turned to look back and see if I was following him. I'd be able to recognize him—in fact—I think I know him—"

"Who do you think this guy is?"

"His name is Richard Fox. He's an attorney with offices in the Hancock Building." O'Neill raised his eyebrows and looked at me. "And why would an attorney be hitting another attorney over the head and rifling through his files?"

"I really don't know, except that Martin Thomas was the US Attorney who tried a case against Fox twenty-five years ago."

The paramedics were leaving with the injured man. One of the paramedics stopped to talk to O'Neill: "We're heading to Northwestern Emergency. Wallet ID's him as Martin Thomas. He's coming around, but looks like he'll have a concussion. He'll be admitted when he gets there if you want to talk to him later."

"Thanks. I'll get his statement after he's been treated," O'Neill said.

A woman in her mid-fifties entered the room. She was in a navy dress and wore dark rimmed glasses. She immediately extended her hand to Officer O'Neill and said, "Hello. I'm Sara Dudley, the building manager. What's happened here? Some of the tenants heard shots and called me. My phone's been ringing off the hook."

"We've had a break-in here. This is Ms. Prince. She witnessed the intruder exit the back door of the office and enter the stairwell.

We figure he's left the building by now and I doubt there's anyone in danger."

"Was anyone hurt in the break-in?"

"Your tenant, Mr. Thomas, is being taken to Northwestern Hospital. I'm going to tape this as a crime scene until we get photos and prints. Office help or anyone else contacts you, you tell them the place'll be reopened as soon as we're done, probably tomorrow," Officer O'Neill said. "Ms. Prince, do you have a local number you can leave with me? We'll want you to come down to the station for a statement now and then you'll be free to go. But I want you to let me know if you're leaving the area."

"I can give you my cell phone number and an office number where you can leave a message for me," I said.

The second officer rejoined us. He had a detective with him. O'Neill asked Sara to wait in the office while the police did their work and lock up the office when they left. We watched for a few minutes as the detective began taking photos of the scene, including the chalk outline on the desk where Martin Thomas had lay sprawled across the files, the file cabinets in the third office that had been opened, and the files on the ground.

I left with Officer O'Neill and retold my story into a tape recorder at the police station on Chicago and Clark. It was eleven o'clock by the time I'd finished at the station. I found myself needing a place to sit and regroup, so I walked the six blocks to Mark's office.

Feeling relatively safe tucked in my temporary office, I thought about the events of the morning. I considered calling Fox, but figured he'd have easily made it back to his place within twenty minutes of leaving Thomas's office, so calling him wouldn't prove anything. There was a strong likelihood that his secretary of thirty years would provide an alibi for him, at least as long as Thomas wasn't seriously injured. But what was Fox after? Maybe the same thing I was, Thomas's files from the 1978 bribery trial.

I called Mark, but his secretary told me he'd be in negotiations all day today. He was undoubtedly working on the contract for the assisted living property. That project would take most of Mark's time for the next six months. There would be land acquisition contracts, title work, construction financing, end loan financing, architectural agreements, construction contracts, employment agreements, partnership agreements, occupancy agreements, operational agreements, and government regulations. Just the thought of all those contracts nearly gave me hives. Thank God I wasn't practicing law anymore.

I called Frank and filled him in on the morning's events. But Frank would have a hard time tying Fox's break-in to George's murder without more evidence. Did I say more evidence? Some would be good. But the more I thought about it, the more this sounded like the closest thing I had to a lead. So I decided to make my way back to Martin Thomas's office on the chance that Fox was forced to leave before he found whatever he was looking for.

Twenty minutes later I was standing in front of Thomas's office door. Yellow crime scene tape ran from top left to bottom right and vice versa across the front door. I walked down the hall to an unmarked door, which I was guessing was the back door to the office. I put on my gloves again and tried the door. Locked. I figured I could get the office manager to let me back in on the pretext that I'd left my briefcase in the office this morning. But I really didn't think I could get her to let me go through the files. I went back and tried the front door. Locked, too. OK, so I'd have to have her let me in.

Luckily, Sara Dudley was in her office and she remembered me.

"In all the excitement this morning, I left my briefcase in Mr. Thomas's office. I really need the papers that are in it. I was wondering if you could let me in, just to get the briefcase?"

"There's police tape on the door. I don't think I'm supposed to let anyone in there until they take that tape off the door."

"Oh please. It'll just take a minute and I really need those papers. We can use the back door and you can come with me. I'll only be a minute."

"Well, I guess we were both in there this morning, so I suppose it would be all right. If we use the back door we won't have to move any tape."

"Great. Thanks so much."

We took the elevator to the twentieth floor and during the ride I learned that Thomas had been a tenant in the office for the past ten years. He'd had a partner for part of that time, but had been a solo practitioner for the past five years.

Sara unlocked the back door to the office and I made a show of searching for my non-existent briefcase. "I thought I put it down in Mr. Thomas's office when I saw him. The shock, you know. I must have put it down because I took his pulse. I don't think I took it with me when I left with Officer O'Neill, but now I don't see it here. Maybe the second officer took it—" I said. "That's probably what happened. Either that or I did take it and left it at the station. I'll go down there now. I'm so sorry to trouble you, Ms. Dudley," I said, making my way to the back door. I reached in my purse and took out two of my cards. I gave one to her saying, "If by any chance it shows up, please call me."

"Certainly. I expect you'll find it at the police station though."

"Yes, you're probably right," I said, opening the back door for Sara to exit. I'd palmed the second card and as I closed the office door I slid the card between the lock and the door jam. I figured it would stay there until the door was opened again, which I planned to do as soon as I left her.

We waited for separate elevators, since Sara Dudley's office was above Thomas's and I was ostensibly going down to the lobby. Sara's elevator came first and, as soon as the doors closed, I hurried back to Thomas's office and let myself in. There was no way for anyone in the hall to see into the office, so I took a chance and turned on the office lights. I slipped on the leather gloves I had in my jacket pocket and opened the file drawers. Files in the first two cabinets were arranged alphabetically. Looking through a few files, I noticed that the correspondence was dated this year. Figuring there might be a chronological order to the cabinets, I moved to the last file cabinet. This seemed more promising. Files here dated back to the early seventies. I opened the next cabinet. Bingo! I found files dated in the mid to late seventies. The documents in the files were copies, no original documents. That made sense, since the actual case files would belong to the US Attorney's office. It appeared that Thomas had made notes of his cases for his own personal records. I looked through the "F's" and—bingo again!—the Fox file was still here. I took the file to the copier and made copies of the twenty-some pages of handwritten notes. It felt like each copy was taking forever, and I couldn't wait to get out of there. Finally the copies were made. I put them in my purse and returned the file back to the cabinet. I closed the drawer, turned off the lights, and let myself out of the office. Waiting for the elevator, I pulled up the collar on my coat and prayed that I wouldn't run into Sara Dudley. When the elevator doors opened on the lobby, I quickly made my way out to the street and blended into the crowd on the sidewalk.

I walked back to Mark's office as quickly as I could. Once in my office, I settled in to look at the copies I'd made from Thomas's files.

The handwritten notes I'd copied were apparently made by Thomas at the time he was handling the Fox case. As I read the notes, the story of George Almonte's changing testimony unfolded. Apparently, when George was interviewed by the US Attorney's office, he'd said he'd overheard a conversation between a judge and Richard Fox in their law office. George said he'd come into the office on a Saturday morning to catch up on some paperwork. He rarely came in on the weekends and he was surprised when he heard two voices. He recognized Fox's voice and listened for a minute. George said the voices became heated and he wondered what was going on. He heard someone ask for an "increase in fees" and, after some argument, he heard Fox say, "All right, Judge, all right." George said he'd quietly walked out of his office and looked into Fox's office. He saw the man Fox was arguing with. George didn't recognize him at the time, but later saw his picture in the paper and identified the man as Judge Zenera. The US Attorney's office figured they had their case in the bag. Then, during the trial, George came to Thomas and said he was no longer sure who he'd heard talking in the office or what kind of fees they were arguing about. George said he'd felt pressured into making the earlier statements and, on reflection, he felt he'd been jumping to conclusions. However phony that may have seemed to the prosecutors, it blew a huge hole in their case. Thomas's notes said the prosecutor's office decided not to call George because his testimony would only confuse the jury. It might even cast suspicion on the whole investigation in the jurors' minds. The prosecutors were left with only a circumstantial case and the jury felt there was enough doubt not to convict.

Thomas's notes said he thought Almonte had just changed his mind about testifying against his partner. I wondered about George's motives. I wondered why Fox had taken such a risk this morning to get this file. And I wondered if George had been blackmailing Fox all these years. But Fox had been acquitted. Double jeopardy would prevent Fox from being tried again for the same crime. So even if George had some evidence against Fox, Fox couldn't have been tried again for that crime. Then it hit me. It wouldn't have been the same crime that Fox was worried about, it would have been perjury! Fox had testified in his own defense. He'd testified that the two thousand dollar withdrawals from his bank account were for his own expenses and he denied he had engaged in any bribery. If George had specific evidence of bribery, he could have been blackmailing Fox with that evidence. That was it. I knew it in my gut. But this all happened more than twenty years ago. Why would Fox kill George now?

As I closed the file, I realized I was exhausted. I didn't feel like going out tonight. I left Mark a note that I'd meet him at home and walked the mile back to his condo.

Chapter 18

Max

I woke up early Thursday morning and thought about Max. Darlene had said he'd be staying at the Ritz and I decided to give him a call. Maybe I could talk to him this morning before the funeral. The operator put me through to Max Almonte's room and Max answered on the second ring.

"Max, this is Karen Prince."

"Yah."

Charming, I thought. But I said, "I'm a friend of Alice Almonte."

"Yah."

"First, let me say I'm so sorry for your loss."

"Thanks, but I'm all right. Is that why you called?" This fellow wasn't spending his time at the clinic in any communications skills studies, that's for sure.

"I called to talk to you. I'm trying to help Alice."

"What's the matter with Alice?"

"I thought you might have heard. She's been arrested for your father's murder."

"I did hear that, but I don't see how I can help."

"Well, maybe you know something that will help clear her. I was wondering if you'd meet with me."

"I don't see when. I'm flying out tomorrow. I'm here to meet with the attorneys and go to the funeral. That's it."

"I'll only take a few minutes of your time. We can talk over breakfast. It'll be my treat," I said.

From what I'd heard, Max was always looking for a handout, so I thought the free breakfast might appeal to him. And sure enough it did. He took the bait.

"Yah, all right. But you have to come over here. I'll meet you in the restaurant in the Ritz in a half hour."

"Fine. I'll be there."

95

That meant a bit of scurrying for me, but I figured I could make it. I jumped in and out of the shower and threw on my black suit and pumps for the funeral. I did my streamlined version of makeup—mascara and lip gloss—and kissed Mark goodbye, saying I had to run and I'd call him later this morning.

The Ritz is located four blocks away from Mark's place. It's on the sixth floor of the Water Tower, the original of the now numerous glitzy shopping center/office/condo high rise complexes on the Mag Mile. I entered the white marble building on Pearson, using the entrance for the hotel east of the shopping center entrance. The ground floor lobby had a huge floral bouquet and an oriental carpet to set the tone of elegance and refinement. This was just the entry to the elevators that would carry me to the sixth floor which held the registration lobby, the Ritz's restaurant called The Dining Room, and the lounge.

I rode the wood-paneled elevator up and found my way to The Dining Room. The maitre d' took my coat and seated me at a table overlooking the small park just to the south of the Water Tower Building. I told him I was expecting a guest and, within five minutes, the maitre d' escorted an excruciatingly thin blonde young man to my table.

"You're Max, I presume?"

"That's me."

"I'm Karen Prince," I said, extending my hand. I was surprised by the delicacy of Max's hand. It was small, almost feminine. He was about five foot six, my height.

"So, Karen, how's Alice?" he asked.

"She's still in the hospital. The doctor thinks she'll be able to go home in a few days."

"Hospital? Why's she in the hospital?" he asked, looking surprised.

"A neighbor found her passed out on her bed two nights ago. There was an empty pill bottle on her bedside table."

"Oh geeze, I hadn't heard that. Do they think she's going to be all right?"

"They think so. But the State's Attorney thinks she tried to kill herself out of guilt and will use it against her in the trial."

"It sort of looks like it though, doesn't it?" he asked.

"Well, I certainly don't think Alice killed your father. Do you?"

"You know, I don't know what to think. My old man was a son-of-a-bitch and he treated Alice, and everyone else who loved him, like dirt."

"Including you?" I asked.

"Definitely. I had to go into a rehab program I don't need just so he'd give me what is rightfully mine anyway."

"What was he giving you?"

"A measly three hundred thousand dollars is what. And for that, I'm supposed to spend six months of my life in a hospital. What kind of father does that to his son?"

"Why did you agree to it?" I asked.

"I wanted the money for a down payment. I'm buying a house. I was getting married. You'd think he'd be happy, but no—he goes ballistic. Says I need a drug rehab program. I'm not even using drugs."

"So why did you go into the program if you're not using drugs?"

"To get the money for our house, just like I said. Dale wanted a house if we were going to be married."

"I hadn't heard you were married. Congratulations," I said.

"Yah. We just went to Vegas and did it and then I went into this program six weeks ago. Four more months and I would have had my money and my new house."

"And now?"

"Now, well, now I guess I'll get my house a little sooner."

"You don't sound too broken up about your father's death."

"I'm not. We didn't get along. And everyone knows that. I don't have to explain myself to you or anyone else."

"So it's really sort of convenient for you that your father is out of your way?"

"Yah, but I didn't kill him, if that's what you're implying," Max said, glaring at me. Suddenly he threw down his napkin and stood up.

"I'm not accusing you," I said, shocked by his outburst. "Please sit down."

"I don't think so," he said and stormed out.

Well, that hadn't gone quite as I'd expected.

The waiter came by with a silver coffee urn and began pouring. I let him fill my cup, but asked him not to fill the other and to bring the check.

At least I learned that Max was married, for whatever that was worth.

It was only nine o'clock, so I walked over to my office at Mark's firm and called Alice. She was able to talk now and was clearly shaken by everything that had happened.

"Alice, how are you doing?"

"Been better," she said.

"Doctor tells me you'll be home in a few days."

"They want to keep an eye on me. But really, I feel like I could recover better at home."

"Well, I don't think you should leave. You've been through an ordeal and if they'll let you stay there and rest, then you should do just that."

I expected the doctors wanted to evaluate her and be confident she wasn't going to do herself in the minute she got home.

"You know, Karen, I can't remember a thing about the other night. I mean, I know I was tired and went to bed sort of early, but I don't remember taking any pills. In fact, I don't remember even thinking about taking them—that scares me."

"The doctors say memory loss isn't uncommon after such a traumatic event—and it could be from the amount of drugs in your system."

"Karen, I have to tell you something—don't think I'm crazy, but––I keep feeling like I didn't do it."

"Of course you didn't," I said, thinking she was talking about the murder.

"No, I mean—I didn't take the drugs—I didn't try to kill myself."

"Alice, Louise found you there with the pills by your side."

"I know, I know. But it just doesn't make sense to me. I was upset, but not like that. I wouldn't kill myself. After all, you're getting me out of this mess, aren't you?"

"Yes, of course," I said, with more confidence than I felt. "Get some rest and I'll check in with you later," I said.

"Not much else I can do here sweetie," she said and laughed. This was the first laugh I'd heard from her since Saturday and I figured it was a good sign. We hung up and I checked my watch.

I still had a few hours before George's service. I turned on my computer and went online to make my travel arrangements for tomorrow's trip to California. With a few keystrokes, I made reservations for a car to pick me up at Mark's at five tomorrow morning. I'd fly out at seven-twenty. Once in LA, I'd rent a car and should get to the Institute about two. That would give me some time to talk to the staff before I met with Doctor Wilson on Saturday morning.

Next, I checked in with Frank, who was now back at his Chicago office. I filled him in on my plans to meet with the doctor in California and about the events in Martin Thomas's office. Frank said he'd schedule an interview with Richard Fox and see what he could learn. Frank made a comment about a psychiatric evaluation for Alice. It sounded like he was thinking of a psychiatric defense as a backup and I didn't like that at all. I knew we'd have to have some concrete evidence if he was going to get Alice acquitted.

I grabbed lunch at my favorite Italian sandwich place. It's tucked away in the courtyard on the lower level of the Hancock Building Plaza. I sat at one of the outside tables, watched other people lunching, and listened to the cascade of water in the courtyard's modernistic fountain. With the ambient city noise, I almost missed the ring of my cell phone.

Grabbing the phone from the bottom of my purse, I flipped the top up and pressed the phone to my ear. Assuming my usual outdoor cell phone position, I covered my free ear with one hand and said, "Hello," hoping I'd be able to hear the caller.

"Karen, dear, is that you?"

"Yes, who is this? I'm in a noisy spot and it's a bit hard to hear."

"Karen, it's Marshall." It was my gallery in New York.

"Marshall. How are you? It's so nice to hear from you."

"Thank you, darling. Your work is doing wonderfully here. We had a reception last night and the Herbnicks love your *Irises*."

"Great, Marshall. That's always nice to hear."

"The reason I'm calling, dear, is to ask you to take a look at a piece a client of ours just bought at auction in London."

"Sure. What's your time frame? I'm in Chicago right now and heading to California on Friday." I occasionally appraise paintings for the gallery. I've become somewhat known for my expertise in the arcane field of Dutch floral paintings from 1600 to 1720. It's an area of knowledge that grew out of research into techniques for my own paintings, which are often in this same style. Over the years I've spoken at various museums and universities and I've come to be known by the few galleries that deal in works from this period.

"Hmm. Well, how about if I email you a digital image and we can talk when you take a look."

"What's the subject of the painting?"

"Lilies, delphinium and paperwhites with butterflies, in a tall crystal vase on a dark wooden table, with a blue-gray background."

"Is it signed?" I inquired.

"No signature. That's one thing that puzzles me. It's a very refined, finished piece. Don't know why the artist wouldn't have signed it."

"And I assume you think it's Dutch seventeenth century, if you're asking me to look at it for you?"

"That's what the auction house implied to our client. But they weren't confident enough of the provenance to make any representations. Apparently they acquired it from a young American who was settling his uncle's estate in London. The young man said his family had originally been from Amsterdam. The frame looks Dutch, I'd say circa 1650.

"Well, email me the image. I'll take a look and call you."

"That's great darling. You are a wonder."

"Thanks, Marshall. I'll talk to you later. It may not be until seven or so, when I'm home."

"Talk to you then."

I flipped the phone shut, packed up my plate and napkin in the white paper sack, tossed them into the black covered trash bin near the stairs, and headed up, back to the Mag Mile. I walked the seven blocks to Drakes with a slight sense of dread. I hated funeral services and I really had no idea what to expect from this one for George.

Chapter 19

Services for George

As I entered the one-story brick building, I was greeted by a gray haired man wearing a dark suit. He escorted me to a smallish sort of living room decorated in various shades of beige. There were sofas and stuffed wing chairs along the walls, forming a circle. Darlene was sitting on the sofa along the wall opposite the door. For a minute I thought I was seeing double. Max sat to Darlene's left, dressed in a black suit. Holding Max's hand was a woman who looked so much like Max I wondered if there was a sister I didn't know about. She was blonde and as thin as Max, with the same pale blue eyes and pointed features. To Darlene's right was David Canter, in a black suit as well. I was actually surprised he owned one. It seemed out of character. There were about twenty other people gathered in the room.

I went up to Darlene and gave her my condolences. I said a wary hello to Max. To my surprise, he stood, shook my hand, and calmly introduced me to his wife, Dale. She seemed to be about Max's age and, when she stood to meet me, I saw she was about his height. We made a few awkward scripted comments and I made my way to a seat on the opposite wall. I guessed most of the people in the room to be former business associates of George's. There was also a small group of women I figured were his horse riding buddies.

Another gentleman in a dark suit entered the room. He stood in front of the fireplace and introduced himself as the director of the funeral home. He began the service by introducing George's family: Darlene, Max and Dale. Next, he read a short statement about George's life, and then led the group in a non-denominational prayer. Organ music floated into the room and, at the conclusion of the music, the Director invited all of the attendees to Darlene's for cake and coffee. That was short and relatively painless, as these services go.

We filed out of the room and made our separate ways the eight blocks to Darlene's. Darlene, Max, and Dale climbed into the black limo waiting for them. A few people decided to brave the parking challenge and went to their cars. I flagged a taxi and arrived just behind the limo trio.

Entering Darlene's home together, we all climbed the stairs to the second floor, where the caterer had set plates of sandwiches, cakes, cookies, and coffee on the long dining room table. An open bar was set up in the living room. I saw Polly standing across the room. Catching her eye, I nodded a hello.

She came over to me and said, "I told Darlene I'd stay here during the service for George. Not smart to leave the house empty. I've heard stories where burglars watch the obituaries for service times and rob the house while the family's burying their dead. Anyway, tell me, how are you doing on your investigation?"

"Nothing much yet," I said.

"And how is Alice?"

"Well, she's still in the hospital, but I talked to her this morning and she sounds better."

"This must all have been too much for her—the divorce, and now this murder."

"It is shocking, but taking pills just seems out of character for Alice."

"Who knows what another person is feeling? Maybe she was just so depressed, it seemed the only way out."

"I don't buy it. She's more of a fighter than that," I said.

"Well, maybe she did it, have you considered that?" Polly asked.

I stared at her. If she was thinking this, then so were most of the people here. "I just know in my heart she couldn't have done it," I said. After a moment's silence, I asked, "Polly, what do you know about a lawyer named Martin Thomas?"

"You mean the one who was attacked in his office?"

"So you heard the story?"

"Hearing about things is my business, darling. I also heard he's writing a book about his trials, sort of a lawyer's memoir thing. He tried some pretty high profile cases as a US Attorney and I guess he figured it would make an interesting book, as well as a pretty good retirement plan."

"Did you know I was the one who found him?"

"What! No I didn't! What were you doing there?'

"Well, I thought he might be able to tell me what had gone on with George's testimony in the Rich Fox case. But someone got to him before me."

"Well, that's one they can't pin on Alice," she said.

"That's right and I know who did do it, too."

"Who?" she asked, clearly surprised.

"Richard Fox."

"How do you know that?" she asked, her voice a high whisper.

"I saw him—I've already told the police," I said.

"What do you think he was doing?" she asked, whispering again.

"I think he was trying to get the files on his case and, with what you've just told me, I'd say he was trying to scare Thomas. I imagine a book on the bribery trial was the last thing Fox wanted. He'd put it behind him and didn't want that mess dredged up all over again," I said.

"So, do you think this ties in with George's murder?" Polly asked.

"I don't know, maybe. The police ought to find out what Fox was doing the night George was murdered. If they don't, Frank will in his interview," I said.

We stood in silence again for a moment. Then Polly changed the subject saying, "I have some ideas for your new Board for the Foundation. I've talked to four people: Marcia Carpenter, Sara Orario, Will Bensky, and Pat O'Brian. They all think it's a great idea. Three of them would definitely agree to serve on your Board and I could probably get all four of them." Polly filled me in on their backgrounds. They sounded like they'd be good board members and I agreed she should send them more information. I authorized Polly to prepare an introductory pamphlet on Turning Points. She said she'd have a sample for my approval in about a week.

"Thanks, Polly," I said.

"My pleasure," she replied.

I thought Polly would be a good Board member herself and decided to play with that idea a bit before asking her to join the Foundation.

Polly and I said our goodbyes and I went looking for Darlene. I found her next to Canter in the den. They were standing in front of the fireplace and Canter was apparently giving some of George's horse riding pals some stretching exercises for before and after riding sessions. I stood by the buffet and watched David and Darlene for a few minutes. Although they never touched, they seemed very connected.

I sensed more than saw someone standing next to me. I turned to find Max standing with a plate of small sandwiches and cookies. Dale joined him with a plate of her own. I wondered why Max had come over by me, but out loud I just said, "Hello."

"Well, I'm glad that's over," he said. He still wasn't showing signs of grief for the loss of his father, at least not to me.

"Yes, funerals are never pleasant events. I'm not sure why the custom persists, since no one likes them," Dale said.

"Acknowledgement," I offered. "It's an acknowledgement of the deceased, of their passing, of support for the surviving family members."

"I suppose," Dale said, sounding more bored than convinced.

Max listened, looked from one of us to the other, and said, "It's all B.S. as far as I'm concerned." Then he walked away leaving Dale and me to stare after him.

I got the feeling that Max enjoyed creating these dramatic little scenes. I talked to Dale for a few minutes and learned she was a California native and had met Max at USC. They'd dated on and off for the past five years, easing their way into marriage and commitment. When our conversation waned, I excused myself and slipped back into the front room to retrieve my coat. Max caught my eye as I was leaving, but didn't come over. I let myself out and headed for Mark's condo.

Chapter 20

Homeward Bound

I walked the two blocks east to Lakeshore Drive and headed south for Michigan Avenue. I decided I might as well take a few extra minutes and pick up the dress I'd bought at Neiman's the last time I was in town. I entered Neiman's familiar red brick arch entrance and took the escalator up to the second floor. Phyllis, my shopping lady, greeted me and retrieved the dress from the alterations department for me in a matter of minutes. I left the store using the side entrance which let me out on Chicago Avenue just across from Water Tower Park. I like taking the short cut through this little park. In fact, I plan my city walks to go through green spaces whenever I can.

I was walking through the park, looking up at the Ritz in the Water Tower where I'd had my morning's aborted breakfast meeting, when a shot rang out. A bullet went by my head and blew away a large part of an oak tree trunk lining the walkway. I screamed involuntarily and turned and crouched, in one fluid motion. I scrambled behind a nearby park bench, but with its open slats, it provided limited protection. I scooted behind the tree next to it. I realized I was holding the handles of my shopping bag so tightly my nails dug into the palm of my hand.

This is a small park, visited by nannies in the afternoon with their small charges and used by a few pedestrians as a pleasant shortcut to the Streeterville area. The nannies had gone and the few other pedestrians now ran for their lives. People across the street at Water Tower looked for a minute, but probably assumed a car had backfired and, after a moment's pause, continued into the shops and on their way. I peeked out from behind my tree, but the park looked empty. I didn't know if the shooter had fled or was waiting for a better shot, but I figured my odds were better to run while whoever was shooting might think he was being watched. I got into a sprinter's starting position, clutched my bag to my chest, and jetted for the park exit. The street sounds disappeared as I listened only for the sound of a shot—none came. I kept running—through the park and right into the adjacent street. A taxi blared its horn and swerved to miss me. Adrenaline propelled me forward—I didn't stop until I was standing in the entry of the Ritz Carlton. I was shaking uncontrollably, gasping for air. I looked around, but I didn't see anyone following me.

I steeled my nerves, walked to the door, and scooted into the first taxi in the cab line. Slumping down in the back seat, I took a five from my purse and handed it to the driver, asking him to take me the two and a half blocks to Mark's condo.

My heart was still pounding as I left the taxi and hurried into the lobby. I hit the elevator button impatiently and furtively studied the man waiting for the elevator with me. Even though my rational mind told me he couldn't have been connected with the shooting in the park, I was still relieved when he got off the elevator.

Once in Mark's condo, I poured myself a glass of Macallan's. Gradually my heart returned to some semblance of normal. Mark wouldn't be home for at least an hour. I decided to use the time to pack for tomorrow's early morning trip.

I planned to be in California only one night so I didn't need much. Underwear and a clean blouse would do. I'd wear a suit I kept at Mark's for business meetings in the city. A large T shirt would double as the night's sleepwear and the morning's exercise gear. I added a pair of shorts and my walking shoes to the carry on. I left the suitcase open with my toiletries bag on top, hoping I'd remember to put it in the suitcase after I used it at four-thirty the next morning.

Packing complete, I started my laptop and updated my notes on George's possible murderers. Fox was looking more and more like a strong candidate. Thinking of Fox made me wonder how Thomas was doing, so I called the hospital. The patient information operator told me that Martin Thomas had been discharged this afternoon. Good for him. And good for Fox, too. At least he wouldn't be facing murder charges in that case.

I put a call into Officer O'Neill to tell him about the Water Tower Park event. He wasn't there and I left a message on his voice mail. I told him I'd be leaving tomorrow morning and expected to be back late Saturday.

Chapter 21

Butterfly Bouquet

After the events in the park, I'd almost forgotten about Marshall's call. I signed onto AOL on the laptop, opened the email from him, and downloaded the image he'd sent. I couldn't believe what I was seeing. I knew this work—and it wasn't by a Dutch painter. I had created this painting, or one just like it, some fifteen years ago. But I had signed mine in the lower right corner, and Marshall had said his painting was missing a signature. And I hadn't put it in an antique frame. I called Marshall and caught him at the gallery.

"Marshall, it's Karen."

"Karen, did the image come through all right?"

"Yes, I was able to open it. But I think there's been some sort of mistake."

"What do you mean?"

"Marshall, this is either a painting I did in the late eighties or copy of my work that someone else did."

"No!"

"Yes! I remember the piece very well. The crystal vase in the painting belongs to a New York collector and friend of mine, who loaned it to me for the painting. I can't imagine how my work came to be in London or in the frame you described. The image you sent didn't show the frame, but I know I didn't use antique frames back then. I had a custom framer doing gold gild here in Chicago."

"Karen, this is incredible, but—there's no signature. Wouldn't you have signed it?"

"Yes, I would have signed it on the ledge of the table. That's where I sign all of my paintings that have an exposed ledge."

"Oh, the Morgans are going to be so disappointed—"

Silence as I digested the fact that someone would be disappointed to know I was the artist who had created this piece.

"No, sorry darling, they loved the work, obviously, I just mean they paid a huge premium for the piece because they thought it might be an undiscovered Rachel Ruysch! Of course they knew they were taking a gamble, but—oh, I hate to be the one to tell them—"

"Uh-huh." Marshall wasn't making any points with me.

"Is there anyway you could look at the work in person and be absolutely certain that this is your work before I get back to the Morgans?" Marshall had a pleading tone in his voice.

"Marshall, I'm sorry. As I said, I have to be in LA on Friday. And I'm in the middle of something important here and I really don't know how long this is going to take—it's sort of hard to say when I could get to New York."

"No, no, I'll get the painting to you, darling. You say you'll be in LA on Friday—I'll have it delivered to our LA gallery. They'll run it up to you." The Morgans must be great clients for Marshall to go through all of this effort and anxiety.

"All right. But I land at LAX on Friday and head down to Laguna from the airport. I'll be back in LA to fly out on Saturday. How about if we set a time for Saturday, say one o'clock? And I'll go to the gallery. It'll be easier. That way if my time frame changes, I won't have to worry about someone waiting for me somewhere."

"Karen, you're an angel! Thank you, thank you, thank you! The painting will be at our LA gallery anytime after four tomorrow. I'll crate it and drop it off myself tonight."

"Aren't you working late?"

"Gallery owner's work is never done my dear—never done."

"Oh—address. Marshall, what's the address and phone at the LA gallery? I know I've been there, but it's been, what, five years since we had the show there?"

"It's 10000 Wilshire, dear. And Andre will have the painting and be waiting for you whenever you get there. Give me a call while you're there. You have my cell, right? Here's my other line. You can always reach me on this, just in case I'm not here."

I wrote Marshall's cell numbers and the gallery info in my little black note book and rang off. I looked at the painting for a few minutes and studied the composition and the colors. Not bad. That's one thing about being an artist. You don't get to see your own work very often after it leaves your studio. And it's rather like seeing an old friend when you get the opportunity. I looked forward to seeing *"Butterfly Bouquet"* in a few days.

It was late enough now that there was a chance Mark would be in his office, so I called and was glad to hear his voice. "Hey there, how's the detecting going?" he said.

"Must be going pretty well, judging by the fact that someone took a shot at me in Water Tower Park today," I said.

"What! Are you all right? Where are you? Did you call the police?" Mark rapid fired questions at me.

"Yes, your place, and yes," I said.

"Karen, this is getting to be too dangerous. I think you should back off and leave this to the police," Mark said and I could tell he was serious.

"And they'll leave Alice in jail for the rest of her natural life," I countered.

"Well, call in a detective if you want, but get yourself out of this investigation. Besides, the fact that there are shots being taken at you while Alice is in the hospital should put her in the clear."

"Yes, if the police believe me and if they think the shots are related to my investigation. They may think it's tied in with the incident at Martin Thomas's office. In fact, maybe it is."

"Do you have any witnesses to the shooting?" Mark asked.

"There were a few people in the park, but everybody ran for their lives. No one was thinking about filing reports when it was going on. And now it's too late," I said.

There was a moment's silence while Mark thought about this. Then he said, "Maybe we can get this on the news and ask anyone who was there to call the police or the news station."

"You know what, that's a great idea. Polly should have some news contacts. I'll give her a call and see what she can do."

"Great. Now wait there. I'll be home in a few minutes," Mark said.

"Good, we need to make it an early night. I have to get up at four-thirty to catch my flight," I said.

"Hmm, I have plans for this evening—I've been thinking about them all day. I think I'd better hurry home if we're going to get any sleep tonight at all," Mark said, a smile in his voice.

I gave a soft laugh into the phone and said, "I'll see you shortly then."

"You certainly will," he said, somehow conveying more than the mere words.

Chapter 22

California

Four-thirty came early.

It had been a restless night. Mark and I finally dozed off about midnight. You'd think I'd have slept like a rock, but I kept having strange dreams that would wake me in a cold sweat. In one, I was walking down a long dark stairway when, suddenly, I was being shot at. I ran down the stairs and out a door onto a street I didn't recognize. I ran into a store and the clerks ducked behind their counters. Then Mark rode through on a huge black horse. But he couldn't see me for some reason. He was calling out and I was so frustrated that he couldn't hear me or see me. I woke with that sense of frustration still filling my mind and looked at the glow of the clock on the bed stand next to me. Four-fifteen. There was no point in going back to sleep now. Mark was lying on his side, turned away from me. I eased out of bed and made my way to the shower.

The water woke me enough to push me through the morning rituals. Promising myself I'd grab a couple hours of sleep on the flight to LA, I toweled off and put on my business suit. No lounging in robes this morning. I put on my makeup and dried my hair, hoping the blow dryer wouldn't wake Mark. I looked older in the mirror this morning. The fluorescent light didn't help and the lack of sleep added a purple color under my eyes. I covered this with makeup and applied mascara and shadow for the bright eyed look. I threw the toiletries into my bag and moved to the kitchen for coffee as quietly as I could. The hot black liquid was a tonic for my grogginess. I felt better as I rolled my carry on bag into the hallway and closed the door behind me. It was five o'clock when I went downstairs to meet my ride to the airport.

Ted had been the night doorman at Mark's building for twenty years. He seemed to know everyone in the building, what they did, who was coming and going when. I expect it kept him from complete boredom, as the night gatekeeper to this high rise dwelling. The building was its own little neighborhood, with a grocery store, parking lot, and dry cleaners. These amenities made daily chores easier for the residents, many of whom were professionals working long hours in the Loop. Still, during Ted's ten pm to six am shift the building was pretty quiet. He relied on conversations with the few residents he encountered, and gossip with the daytime staff as they exchanged places, to build his store of knowledge about the residents.

"Hey, Ted. How are you doing this morning?" I asked.

"Fine, Ms. Prince. You're leaving us early this morning. Where are you off to?" Ted replied.

"California, Ted. Got to catch a seven-twenty flight out," I said.

"They say traffic's not too bad this morning. You'll be O.K.," he said and smiled. "You need a taxi?" Ted asked.

"No, my driver should be here any minute."

"Who's picking you up?"

"Chicago Express. They'll be in a black sedan," I said.

"You wait inside. I'll let you know when they get here," Ted offered.

"Thanks, Ted."

"When'll you be back?" he inquired.

"I'll be back tomorrow night."

"Good, don't want you gone too long now, you know," he said and smiled, taking my bag to the outer lobby with him.

I'd been staring at the marble patterns on the walls and thinking about the past few days events for five minutes when Ted came into the inner lobby to tell me my ride was waiting for me.

I thanked Ted and followed him out to the street. Ted opened the limo door for me and he and the driver put my luggage in the trunk.

Ted waved goodbye as the car pulled away from the curb. We left Delaware Street in the darkness and headed for O'Hare Airport.

Traffic sped along on the highway until the Junction. This is the point where the Kennedy splits from the Edens and heads toward O'Hare. Even at this early hour, there was a backup bringing us to a stop about fifteen minutes from the airport.

We inched our way forward and made it to the American Terminal at five-fifty-five. I rolled my carry on into the terminal and checked the flight display. It looked like my flight would be on time. Great! I issued my boarding pass at one of those self serve machines the airlines have instituted, saving about fifteen minutes of waiting in line. I headed to the gate and found my airplane already there and waiting. Good start. It didn't always happen that way these days. Now, if we don't have mechanical problems, I should be at LAX in six hours.

I checked in at the gate, just to make sure the machine check-in had worked. It had. But the airline rep told me she'd just heard our plane was having engine work done on it and she should have an update on our estimated departure time in half an hour. While I know these planes all have work done on them regularly, it still makes me uneasy when the plane I'm going to fly on is being repaired just before take off. I decided to take a walk, get a paper, and have breakfast at Starbucks. What do they do to that coffee to make it taste so good that people will wait in line to get it and pay twice what coffee costs anywhere else? I don't know, but I buy it when I can. This was my small consolation for waiting at the airport.

I bought the Tribune and searched for any mention of the break-in at Thomas's office. Nothing in this issue. Later, I'd do a search on my laptop in case it was covered in an earlier issue. An announcement was made pushing our departure back. I returned to the gate and talked to the agent again. She said the mechanics had determined they could fix the engine problem, so at least we weren't waiting for another plane. We'd be an hour or so late, but, hey, that's just about considered on time these days in air travel.

I passed the time reading the paper and making notes on my laptop. Finally the boarding began. After some waiting, some lining up, some shuffling down too narrow aisles, we were finally all in our seats. The attendants did their walk-through check of the cabin, making sure we'd all buckled our seat belts and raised our seat backs. The plane pushed back, but we continued to wait in this position for what seemed an inordinate amount of time. People began shifting in their seats and looking around. Finally the Captain came on the speaker and told us that the right engine had failed to turn over. I shuddered to hear the words failed and engine in such close proximity. However, the Captain continued, telling us that this was not a major problem. He was having the plane towed back to the gate and would wait for a large fan to push air through the engine to turn it over and get it started. This bit of news just added to my nervousness

113

about air travel these days. I tried to put my fears out of my mind. The Captain sounded confident and I'd had a look at him as he boarded the plane earlier. He was in his late forties, I guessed, and so I figured he had a good number of years of experience to draw upon. I decided to trust him. What else could I do? Sure enough, thirty minutes later, the engines were started and we pushed back once again, this time continuing to the runway. I hoped I'd make it to Beachfront Institute before the day staff left for the weekend. We'd see.

The rest of the flight went smoothly and we ended up landing about two hours later than planned. With the two hour time change, I still arrived in the LAX airport by twelve-thirty Pacific Time.

I figured I'd see what I could learn about the Institute before tomorrow's meeting with Doctor Wilson. So, after renting a car and driving for two hours, I pulled into the gated compound of the Beachfront Institute at three-thirty Friday afternoon.

Chapter 23

The Beachfront

There was a guard house just beyond the entrance gate. I stopped and explained that I had a meeting with Doctor Wilson tomorrow morning and just wanted to be sure I could find my way to his office. A call to the Director's office authorized the guard to let me pass and he gave me directions to the main building. I followed the paved road for a half mile through wooded grounds and came out on a manicured lawn leading to a large white stone mansion. There were two large wings, one on either side of the round pillared entrance. I pulled into the circular drive and a uniformed guard approached my car and opened my car door for me. He took my keys and handed them to a uniformed car attendant. The guard gave me a ticket receipt for my car and directed me to the desk just inside the door of the Institute.

The lobby was white and gray marble, with tall glass doors opening onto a large main parlor. A woman in a white suit took my name and called the Director's office. I was led to a seat in the inner parlor, adjacent to a massive fountain. In the center of the fountain, a large rock outcropping was covered with a cascade of blooming orchids. Jets of water spouted from four positions around the flowers and fell into a large black marble pool filled with brightly colored coi.

At the far end of the lobby, more glass doors opened out onto a terrace. I walked over to the doors and, finding them unlocked, walked out onto the stone terrace. The view was breathtaking. I was perched at the top of a dramatic cliff, falling away to the ocean shore, some seven hundred feet below. Waves crashed onto a rocky beach. A paved walkway made a serpentine path down to the shore. Magenta bougainvillaeas lined the winding path, directing my eyes down to the shore below. I felt a presence next to me and realized I was not alone. Turning my head, I discovered a petite blonde woman in her thirties standing next to me.

"Gorgeous view, isn't it?" she asked.

"Mesmerizing," I replied.

She held out her hand and introduced herself, "Hi, I'm Ruth Rollings, Doctor Wilson's private secretary. You must be Karen Prince."

"One and the same," I said, extending my hand to meet hers.

She had a strong grip and a steady gaze. I expected she knew exactly what was going on at the Institute at all times.

"I'm supposed to meet with Doctor Wilson tomorrow morning, but I just flew in this afternoon, so I thought I'd drive out and be sure I could find my way here."

"Did you have any trouble getting here?" she asked.

"No. The directions on your web site were very clear and I found my way without a problem, thanks. I couldn't resist walking out here to check out the view," I said, turning to look out at the ocean again.

"It's spectacular, isn't it? We own twenty-five hundred acres along the coast here. There are twenty separate living quarters on the grounds for extended stay guests and ten suites here in the main building," she volunteered.

"Are all your rooms filled right now?" I asked.

"Yes, we have quite a waiting list."

"That's a great tribute to Doctor Wilson's work," I said.

"Yes, his patients love him and are extremely satisfied with the results of his programs."

"I know someone, step-son of a dear friend of mine, who's staying here. His name is Max Almonte. How is Max doing?" I asked.

"Oh, so you're a friend of Max's family? Unfortunately, Max had to leave before his work was finished here. Usually we require the patients to live up to their contracts and stay the full agreed upon time, but in his case, given the circumstances, we felt, of course, that it was only right that he return to Chicago," she said solemnly.

"Yes, I saw him there yesterday with his wife."

"How is Max feeling?" she asked.

"Well, given the circumstances I'd say he was doing all right, as far as I can tell," I said.

"Good. He was still feeling ill when he left here on Sunday," she said, concern in her voice.

"Really? I didn't know he was sick. What was the matter with him?" I asked.

"He'd been in bed for days. I think it was Thursday that he started running a fever. He seemed to have the flu," she said. "The doctor looked at him on Thursday, but Max refused any treatment on Friday and Saturday, saying he just wanted to be left alone. His fever had abated and we just let him rest in bed as he wanted."

"I suppose his wife was there with him," I said.

"Well, actually, his wife had a seminar or conference of some sort and was traveling for the weekend," she said.

"Oh, what kind of conference was that?" I asked.

"Well, I wouldn't know. I don't—oh, wait a minute, I think I do know—she said that she was a broker."

"She's a stock broker? She doesn't seem the type," I said.

"No, no, she's a real estate broker."

"Oh. Do you know where the conference was by any chance?"

"I really couldn't say. I've probably already said more than I should. I just figured, your being a friend of the family's—" her voice trailed off.

"I'm sorry, I didn't mean to ask you anything that made you uncomfortable," I said. "I was just wondering because I'm working with Detective Cavanaugh to determine where everyone was the night Max's father was killed." It was a bit of a stretch to say I was working with Cavanaugh, but I figured I sort of was, because Cavanaugh should have been looking into this very thing and I certainly would share whatever I found out with him.

"Oh, I see. Well, it is such a sad thing for Max, never having had a chance to reconcile with his father, and all," she said.

"Yes, it is sad," I said, trying to establish a common viewpoint with her. "Will Max be coming back here soon, do you know?"

"I don't know. He left under such unexpected and sudden circumstances. He left all of his things here and he still has his cabin waiting for him. We hope he'll be back to finish his program," she said.

"Yes, that'd be the best thing for him, I'm sure, especially with his new responsibilities. Tell me, Ms. Rollings, do you think you'd have time to show me around the Institute this afternoon?" I asked.

"Well certainly, and you can tell me a bit about your Aunt Rose while we take our tour," she said.

"Yes, that would be perfect," I said, getting a little nervous about creating a fictional aunt.

"Well, let's start our tour in the main lobby, where you came in," Ruth said and led us back through the glass doors.

"This central lobby is our reception area. Our clients check in here, as do their guests. We keep a registry of everyone coming in and out of the Institute. It's important in the treatment to know with whom our clients are meeting and what influences they might be under. Doctor Wilson sets visitation parameters for each patient depending upon what he feels will be best for the individual."

We continued walking and she said, "Through these doors are our guest suites in the main building. As I said, they're all currently occupied, but I can tell you, they're about two thousand square feet, each with ocean views. They all have a living room, dining room, study, bedroom, and spa-bathroom. We have a central kitchen which prepares all the meals our clients require. Our central dining room is on the other side of the lobby, overlooking the ocean. We find the natural setting here to be very relaxing. There are walking paths and, of course, our exercise and spa facilities. Let's go to the other wing, and I'll show those to you," Ruth said.

As she led us down the hall, she continued, saying, "Tell me about your Aunt Rose."

"Well, Aunt Rose is in her mid-seventies. She's been recently widowed, as I mentioned. The strain of dealing with the estate and being widowed has been a bit much for her. I think it would do her good to just get away for a month or so," I said, spinning the tale I'd worked out on the flight here.

"Where does your Aunt live?" Ruth asked.

"In Chicago, well, Kenilworth, actually. That's a northern suburb along Lake Michigan," I said.

"What did your uncle do?" she asked.

"Oh, Uncle Elmore had retired long ago. His father founded a manufacturing company. Uncle Elmore built the company into an international firm. They had no children of their own to take over the company, so he sold it a few years ago for a fortune," I explained.

"I see, so your Aunt has to manage the investments," Ruth said.

"Yes, and I don't think she was much involved in that when my uncle was alive," I said.

"I can see how that would be stressful, especially at her age," Ruth said, sympathetically.

We had crossed the lobby once again and this time entered the south wing of the main building. "Our administrative offices are in here: accounting, record keeping, that kind of thing. This is our pharmacy. We have a fully staffed pharmacy for our patients' needs."

We walked past offices for the professional staff and several long file rooms.

We turned left and walked down a wide hallway, which led to the ocean side of the building. "Doctor Wilson's office is down here," Ruth said.

We entered a white wood paneled room with a floor to ceiling glass wall facing the ocean. The walls were lined with books and California impressionist paintings of the coastline. The furniture was pristine white and the desk immaculate. Apparently whatever magic Doctor Wilson performed did not involve him in a lot of detailed paperwork. We walked through a door in the far side of the office, which led to another smaller office with the same spectacular view.

So this is where all the paperwork went, I thought. Piles of files were stacked in an in-box and filing cabinets lined the walls.

"This is my office. Please excuse the mess. There's an incredible amount of paper work involved, as you can see," Ruth said, waving her hand in the direction of the files. Naturally, I keep the files in order for Doctor Wilson."

"Are these all patient files?" I asked.

"Many of them are. We keep a detailed account of each patient's activities and progress while they're here. Then there are the operational records for running a place like this. Think of the records you have for your home and then multiply them by a thousand," Ruth said. "Our accounting department maintains those records, but Doctor Wilson reviews all of the financial statements and approves all hiring and expenses. He is a very hands-on operator," Ruth said, smiling. It was clear Ruth Rollings took a great deal of pride in the operation of this facility.

"I see—and you must be a great help to him in that work," I said.

"I do what I can, yes," Ruth said modestly.

I got the feeling that Ruth Rollings had been running this Institute for quite a while now.

119

"You know, I'd really like to see one of the cabins. I know they're full, but couldn't you perhaps just show me Max's since he isn't here? We won't be a minute in there, but I really don't think I could recommend my Aunt stay here if I couldn't see where she would actually be living," I said.

"Well, I don't think Max would mind, your being a friend of the family's and all." Ruth went to her desk and opened the top right hand drawer. She lifted a pencil tray and removed a large key ring from a hidden compartment in the drawer.

Keys in hand, we walked back out to the terrace and turned left. Behind a vine covered wall were three golf carts and a stone pathway.

"These carts are our main mode of transportation on the grounds," Ruth said and motioned me into the seat next to her.

The key had evidently been left in the cart and she reached down to her right and turned it to the on position. The cart started up with a spurt and we headed down the winding stone path into the pine forest to the south of the main building. The stone path gave way to crushed pine needles as we moved under a canopy of tall pines. The path continued into the woods, turning away from the ocean for about a quarter mile. Smaller paths appeared every so often off to our right. These must lead to the guest cabins overlooking the ocean. There are numbered brass plaques at the right hand side of each of these pathways. I assumed these corresponded to the addresses for the cabins. About a half mile along the main path we came to Number 450, and turned down the narrow trail. The path swooped in gentle curves lined with hundred foot pine trees. We came out on a grass clearing, sporting a cabin edged with a manicured garden. Red and white flowers lined the front of the cabin, adding a cheery air. The lawn area was small, with two Adirondack lounge chairs and a table tucked in the farthest corner from the cabin. The cabin itself was natural cedar with the door and window trim painted the rusty color of the fallen pine needles. A woodpecker flew from the nearest tree and butterflies floated from flower to flower in the garden. The afternoon sun shone down on this little clearing and warmed the air.

Ruth steered the cart along the path leading to the front door and turned off the motor.

"This is Max's place.   It's identical to the other cabins," Ruth said, walking up to the front door and pulling the keys from her jacket pocket. She turned the lock and led the way into the cabin.

The interior was all pine paneling, bringing the feeling of the outdoors inside. The living room opened onto the dining room, where large windows looked out toward the ocean. The den opened off the dining room and that, too, had large windows facing the ocean. The cabin was situated near the cliff leading down to the ocean. The main path was far enough away so you would probably never hear carts approaching, unless one came directly up to the door. It was a perfect retreat.

"This is lovely," I said. "Do all your guests drive one of those carts to get to the main building?" I asked.

"Yes, or they can call us and we'll have someone come and pick them up. But most of the guests prefer to drive themselves," Ruth said.

"My Aunt might just prefer the main building then.   Don't know how she'd do driving a golf cart," I said, sounding concerned. "Do you think it'd be possible to see one of the suites in the main building?"

"Well, we do have one suite which our counselors use for therapy sessions.   It'll give you a feeling for the layout, the furnishings and such. Why don't I show that to you?"

"That would be wonderful. Thank you Ruth," I said, sounding relieved.

"Let me just walk through here one more time to get the feel of this place as well, just so I can describe it to Aunt Rose," I said and walked on to see Max's bedroom.   Things seemed orderly.   There were a few items of clothing in the closet and a few personal items on the dresser. I suppose Max had packed his clothes from here for the trip to Chicago. I didn't see any personal diaries or calendars lying around. But I couldn't search the room with Ruth watching me. Still, I got the impression there wasn't much here for me to see. I felt disappointed after my long trip to get here.   Don't know what I expected—maybe a confessional note. Oh well.

I decided to try to get a look at Max's file. Maybe I could find something in there. But I didn't expect Ruth to just hand that over to me, even if I did have a rich Aunt Rose.

"Thanks, this gives me a feel for the cabins, Ruth. Do you think you have time to show me the suite you mentioned in the main building?" I asked.

"Of course, let's go over there right now," Ruth said, smiling.

We left the cabin and Ruth locked the door behind her. I doubted there was anything in there to tie Max to his father's murder, but figured I might be able to come back here later and do a more thorough search.

It took about five minutes by golf cart to get back to the main facility. There seemed to be only the one main path through the woods, so I figured I could find my way back here without difficulty. We entered the building again and Ruth showed me the suite used as a counseling room. I nodded to her comments, asked a few questions to feign interest, and then thanked her for her tour. I told her I would talk with Doctor Wilson tomorrow and be in touch with her after I met with my Aunt. We shook hands and Ruth walked me back to the main lobby.

I walked through the lobby as slowly as I could. When I thought Ruth would be through the lobby and well on her way to her office, I turned around and asked the receptionist if there was a ladies room I could use before the drive to my hotel. She pointed across the main lobby. "There are restrooms just to the right of the doors to the terrace, Ms. Prince," she said.

Darn, she knew my name. Oh well, I was in anyway. I thanked her and walked back across the lobby to the ladies room. On my way out I turned left instead of right, and continued down the hall to the filing rooms I'd passed on my tour. It was after five o'clock now, on a Friday afternoon, and most of the office staff had left for the weekend. I ducked into the first file room, closed the door, and switched on the lights. I went to the far end of the room and opened the top drawer of the cabinet. Quickly glancing at the labels on the manila files, I saw that these were building operation files. I moved to the middle of the room and tried one of the cabinets there. Getting closer. These were patient files. I was in the W's—Weatherspoon, Winters. I closed the drawer and moved closer yet to the front of the file room. C's, Calloway, Caruthers, Chesterfield. Moving two more over, I had it. The A's. Allen, Allister, Almonte. This was it. I pulled the file and quickly opened it. "Patient information" was typed neatly on the left hand side. I jotted down Max's address. Employer was left blank. There was also information on his spouse. Dale's name and address appeared as well as her employer: Bard and Strome Commercial Realtors, 15550 Wilshire Blvd., LA. I jotted down the address and phone number for Bard and Strome and paged through the rest of the file. There was a copy of the admissions contract. There were no notations by counselors or other kinds of evaluation reports. These must be the billing files. Patient counseling files must be kept somewhere else. I heard a phone ring in an office outside the file room. It rang three times and stopped. They were probably on voice mail. I put the file back in its drawer and leaned against the exit door. I turned out the lights and listened for voices or footsteps. It was dead silent. I thought about searching for the counseling file on Max, but decided to check out his cabin first.

I slowly opened the file room door and slipped back into the hallway. I moved quickly back down the hall, retracing my steps to the ladies room. I passed it by and walked back through the lobby and past the receptionist desk, which was now empty. Guess she'd gone home for the weekend as well. The doorman nodded and I handed him the ticket for my car. In a few minutes, a uniformed man brought my car around and held the door open for me. I thanked him and slid into the driver's seat. I drove to the far end of the lot. Here the road forked with one drive leading to a parking area filled with cars, which I guessed was the long term parking area for the guests' cars. The other road was marked as the exit road. Hmm, choices, choices. I pulled my car into the parking lot and tucked it between a Mercedes and a Jaguar. I thought of the flashlight I keep in my own car, but figured the rental car was not as well equipped for nighttime explorations. Too bad. I locked the car and walked back down the road, toward the pine trees, ducking into the woods as quickly as I could.

Chapter 24

Max's Cabin

The late afternoon light already had the reddish glow of sunset and I hoped I'd be able to find my way back to my car in the dark. The pine trees were tall enough to block out most of the light on the forest floor, so undergrowth was practically nonexistent. My feet crunched the pine needles releasing a pleasant odor into the cooling air. I made my way toward the ocean and stumbled onto the cart path. Without the sound of the cart, I could hear the waves crashing on the shore below. I kept my eye out for the paths leading to the cabins and began to jog, hoping to find the marker for 450 before the light got too low. I saw a sign for 600 and kept on the path. A half a mile and three markers later, I came to 450 and turned down the narrow lane.

As I came up to the cabin, I hoped there wasn't an alarm system on the door. I hadn't seen Ruth turn one off, so I was guessing, and hoping, there weren't any alarms on these cabins. I slipped on my gloves, grabbed the door knob, and tried turning it. It was locked, as I had expected. I walked around to the side of the cabin and tried the living room window. It was locked tight. Pooh. I made my way around the cabin and tried each window in succession. Growing up, I'd played softball. Our coach taught us to run out the bases, even if you thought you'd hit a ground ball out. I'd been surprised how many times some intervening force let me get to base. The shortstop let the ball go through her legs. The first baseman missed the catch. Or someone left a window unlocked. Eureka! The bedroom window was opened about three inches. Guess Max liked fresh air when he slept. I pushed the window up all the way. There was a screen in place, but I popped it out easily. I pulled myself up, through the window, and into the cabin.

Screened by the trees from the adjoining cabins, I felt safe turning on the lights. I didn't know exactly what I expected to find, but I figured it didn't hurt to look. I started in the bedroom, going through drawers. A sweater, jeans, and a pair of shorts were in the top drawer.

The second held underwear. Nothing tucked in between the boxer shorts. Bottom drawer was evidently dirty laundry. Well, I was wearing gloves. I moved a few items about and was surprised to find ladies lace panties and bra amongst the sweatshirts and jeans. Conjugal visits? Why leave your clothes here though? I wondered if Dale had stayed here with Max. I would have thought the patients would stay here alone. I'd ask Doctor Wilson about Max's guest restrictions tomorrow.

I moved to the bathroom and went through the medicine cabinet. Pretty sparse, as I guess you'd expect for a temporary residence, which Max wasn't even inhabiting this week. There was an unopened tube of toothpaste, soap, shampoo, and, hey, eye makeup remover. Dale's I assumed, or Max was into stranger things than I thought. I moved to the den and looked through the desk drawers. There was a pad of paper by the phone with an 800 number jotted down. I copied it to try later. There were also some times, and a number—maybe a flight number? I decided not to wait. I pulled out my cell phone and tried the phone number. Sure enough, it was American Airlines. I pressed the zero and was put on hold for a customer service representative. I held the phone with my left hand and continued my search of the desk. On the corner of the desk, there was a stack of books, which consisted of a few paperbacks and magazines. I cradled the phone with my neck and shoulder, hoping I wouldn't inadvertently disconnect myself, and leafed through the books. They didn't appear to contain any clues, not even a bookmark. All I learned was that Max read Agatha Christie. That came as a minor surprise to me. I looked in the desk drawers and found a Chicago phone book. Max must have brought this; don't think they're standard issue in California. The top drawer had a few pens and pencils and a book of matches from an LA restaurant. That was it.

I moved into the living room, but found no personal items, just standard furniture: a sofa, two chairs, and a coffee table, all in a rustic hand hewn wooden look.

The airline rep came on the line and I said, in my nicest voice, "Hi, I'm one of your frequent flyers and I'm wondering if you can help me. I have a flight number that a friend of mine gave me and I can't remember the time she's coming in. It's flight 212. I think it leaves LAX at five–twelve a.m. Do you have the arrival time at O'Hare?"

"Sorry, I don't have a flight 212 into O'Hare in the morning. Let me check something—I have a flight 212 leaving LAX at five-twelve p.m. daily, arriving O'Hare at eleven-thirty p.m."

"Oh, thank you. That's where I was confused. Thanks so much."

"No problem. Thanks for choosing American."

"Bye." Well, I didn't know how I'd use the information, but there it was. Max had apparently flown into O'Hare at eleven-thirty p.m. There were no dates written on the pad, but I assumed this must have been when he and Dale flew in on Monday.

I didn't see anything else of interest in the cabin, so I closed the lights and hefted myself back out the bedroom window. I replaced the screen and pulled the window down to its original position, leaving it open three inches from the bottom.

The sun had set and the woods seemed very dark after the lit rooms of the cabin. I let my eyes adjust to the low light and made my way to the narrow lane back to the main cart path. I was certain I'd get lost if I tried to make my way through the woods off the path in the dark. Anyway, if someone else was on the path, they'd have lights on their cart and I'd be able to duck into the woods before they saw me.

It was a half hour before I made it back to my car. The lot was lit by tall overhead lights and I didn't see anyone else around. I got into the car, started the engine, and headed for the only exit I knew—the one past the guard house. I was furiously thinking of what to tell the guard as I drove to the exit: a fake name?—a meeting with Ruth Rollings? But what if she's left by now and the guard knows that? I'd decided to go with my own name—at least that would match the entry list—and a meeting with Ruth Rollings. I'd have to make something up if she'd already left and the guard caught that.

I pulled up to the white guard house and the guard in a blue uniform and cap poked his head out of the small shelter. I smiled and gave the guard my name. He nodded, made a note, and the white gate swung open allowing me to proceed up the road. That wasn't too bad. I wondered what would happen if one of the guests wanted to leave, but I guess they can. It is a voluntary program.

I headed back up the road I'd come on and stopped at a motel I'd passed on the way in, about fifteen minutes from the Institute. They had a room. The night manager gave me a key and told me there'd be coffee and breakfast in the lobby starting at six a.m.

I wheeled in my suitcase and called Mark. It was two hours later in Chicago and he was home, getting ready for bed. I filled him in on my day and learned that Alice was home and recovering nicely. Louise was checking in on her twice a day and bringing her meals. Alice still insisted she hadn't taken the pills. Mark chalked it up to denial and thought she should be getting some serious counseling, immediately. I agreed. With all she'd been through, counseling was probably a good idea. I told Mark I'd call Alice in the morning or from the plane on my way back. We said we'd see each other tomorrow night and hung up.

I thought about my plans for the next day. I had two more things I wanted to check out while I was here and I hoped to make the last flight out of LAX tomorrow. That would be the same five-twelve p.m. flight that Max had taken. First, there was my meeting with Doctor Wilson; then, I wanted to see what I could learn about Max and Dale from their home and from Dale's office. Oh, and I'd promised to stop at the gallery, too. That meant a lot of driving tomorrow.

I got my maps out and charted my routes. I called the highway patrol and checked on construction. Last thing I needed was to spend hours in stopped traffic. Well, I guess in LA I would be spending hours in traffic however you looked at it, but at least I wanted to avoid construction back-ups.

I got ready for bed, thinking of how I'd get into Max and Dale's home without a key. Since I'd never been there, I had no information on which to base a plan. I'd just have to wait and see what the situation called for when I got there. As I lay down, I didn't think I'd be able to sleep; but once my head hit the pillow, I was out. I guess I was more exhausted than I'd thought.

Chapter 25

Doctor Charles Wilson

My alarm went off at five-thirty and the wakeup call came in while I was getting out of the shower at five-forty-five. I like to have a backup alarm when I'm traveling, since you never know the reliability of the hotel's systems. By six I was dressed and went to the lobby for coffee.

It was a sunny day and looked like a good day for travel. I packed the car, checked out, and headed for the Institute. I'd be early, but I figured I could do a little more exploring while I waited.

By seven I was back at the entry gate explaining to the guard that I had an appointment with Doctor Wilson this morning. He checked his list and waved me in, directing me to the main building. The place had a quiet air about it this morning. I drove into the entry circle and the guard at the front door came out and down the steps. I waited for him in my car and explained that I just wanted to wait in the lobby for my appointment with Doctor Wilson. I told him I'd flown in from out of town and had nowhere else to wait. I could see he didn't want to turn away someone with an appointment with Doctor Wilson, so he directed me to leave my car in the parking area and meet him back at the front door. He apologized that there was no one to take the car for me, explaining that the weekend parking staff didn't arrive until eight.

I made my way to the parking lot and then back to the guard. He let me into the main interior lobby and I settled myself into a comfortable chair. In a few minutes I went back to the guard and asked for directions to the ladies room. I didn't want him wondering where I'd gone when he looked into the lobby and saw I wasn't there. Repeating my trick from yesterday afternoon, I found my way back to the filing rooms.

This time I wanted to find the patient counseling files on Max. The office staff was not around and I assumed they would be out for the weekend. I tried the door next to the filing room I had already been in, but it was locked. Just as a check, I tried the door to the filing room I'd been in yesterday and it was locked as well. The guards must have locked up these rooms after I'd left last night. Darn. Then I thought of the ring of keys in Ruth Rollings' desk drawer and hoped she'd remembered to put the keys back after our little tour yesterday.

I walked down the hall to her office. Thank heavens the office doors were open and I let myself in. The keys were there in her desk drawer, under the pencil tray, where she'd taken them from yesterday. I quickly put them in my purse, replaced the pencil tray, and closed the drawer.

I made my way back to the file rooms and, looking over my shoulder to be sure no one was around, I tried the keys. The fifth one turned the lock and I slid inside. I flipped the light switch and relocked the door. This room looked just like the one I was in yesterday and, for a minute, I thought I'd let myself into the room I'd already searched. I opened a file drawer and looked through the first file. No, this wasn't the same room. These were the counselors' notes on the patients, including their psychiatric evaluations. The file I had was labeled Margaret Barber. I returned the file, closed the drawer, and looked in the next drawer up.

Yes! This one started with Abbott. I quickly looked at the labels on the next files, finding Maxwell Almonte's six files back. I laid the file on the open drawer and read. There were six pages of notes. Each page appeared to be from a separate session with a counselor. The gist of it was that Max was obsessed by feelings of hate toward his father, stemming from feelings of abandonment. He'd been taking drugs for the past four years, mostly prescription antidepressants. He'd begun drinking heavily last year and the stated goal of his stay was to break his alcohol dependency. I couldn't blame George for not wanting to give his son his inheritance while Max had a drinking problem. I read through the other five pages and found more of the same. The good news was that Max had been without alcohol for the duration of his stay.

I slipped the file back into the drawer and checked my watch. Seven-thirty—long time for the ladies room. Oops. I figured I'd better get back and make an appearance at the front lobby. I turned off the light and slipped back into the corridor. I heard footsteps around the corner, coming from the direction of Ruth Rollings' and Doctor Wilson's offices. I quickly dropped the keys into my purse and headed in the other direction. This brought me back to the lobby and I went directly to the front doors to make myself seen by the guard. He wasn't at his station and I wondered if the footsteps I'd heard were his.

I sat on the sofa for a minute and then decided to return the keys to Rollings' office. It would only get harder to do that as the morning wore on and more people were around. I'd have to take my chances with the footsteps. I walked to the ladies room door and lingered there a moment, hoping the guard would walk by and see me here. No such luck. I moved down the hallway and made my way to Doctor Wilson's office. I ducked in and walked through the connecting door to Rollings' office. Both offices had glass exterior walls with blinds drawn up to expose the ocean view. The interior walls were drywall, so I could only be seen by someone outside or from the doorway. I moved quickly behind Rollings' desk and dropped the keys into their secret compartment in the first drawer. I was just walking out of the room when the guard came in.

"Hi," I said. "I was just looking for my earring—I was here yesterday and I thought I might have dropped it when I met with Ruth." I thought using her first name would make me sound like I was on close terms with Rollings. That might give me some dispensation for being in her office.

The guard stared at me. He didn't like the fact that I'd been snooping around, but he also didn't know quite what to do with me.

"Uh-huh. Well, the cleaning people were through here last night. Why don't you come back to the front lobby with me and tell me what the earring looked like. I'll check with the cleaning crew when they come in," he said.

"Oh, sure, that sounds like a good idea," I said and followed him back to the lobby. I made up a small, gold, clip-on earring and resumed my wait on the lobby sofa.

It was a quarter to eight by now and I spent the next fifteen minutes doing stretches and isometrics while I waited for Doctor Wilson.

The director arrived on time, dressed in a white golf shirt and khaki pants. The guard spoke to him for a few minutes, but I could

only watch their pantomime behind the lobby glass doors. I
wondered if the guard was telling the good doctor about my hunting
expedition, but there was no way for me to know. I tried to read
Wilson's body language as he approached me and didn't think the
guard had mentioned finding me in Rollings' office. Most likely he'd
just have told the doctor that I'd arrived early and he'd had me wait in
the lobby. What would he have said, "She went to the bathroom for a
really long time and I found her looking for an earring in Rollings'
office?" Maybe, but I didn't think so. It didn't put the guard in a
very good light either.

"Good morning, Ms. Prince," Doctor Wilson said, extending his
hand.

I rose and we shook hands. Firm grip. Good. I hate those fingertip
grips so many men give women.

"Good morning, Doctor Wilson. Call me Karen, please," I said.

"Fine, Karen then. How was your trip? Found your way here
without problem?" he asked.

"Yes. I flew in yesterday and, in fact, I came here and met with
Ruth Rollings. She's already given me a splendid tour of your
facility. So, I just had a few questions about the Institute and your
policies, if you wouldn't mind."

"Not at all, of course. Tell me about your Aunt—Rose, isn't it?"

"Yes, her name is Rose Cummings. I was talking to a friend who
told me about your Institute and it sounded like the perfect retreat for
my Aunt. Maybe you could help her with adjusting to her new
responsibilities and widowhood. It's all quite a lot for her to absorb,
you know. It's very important that she stay alert, what with all the
financial matters she'll have to manage now."

"How old is your Aunt?"

"Seventy-five. She's quite alone, you see, except for me."

"Is she seeing a doctor at home?"

"No. Of course, she has her regular physician, but she's in
excellent health and under no psychiatric treatment. But, I do think
she is drinking a bit more sherry than she has in the past," I said,
raising my eyebrows.

"I see. We have excellent counselors here, if that's what you're
interested in for your Aunt."

"Yes, it is, and the setting is beautiful. I think that would make it feel more of a vacation for her. I was wondering if I could visit her while she's here?"

"I determine the visitation policy that best suits each patient, but I would think it would be helpful for your Aunt to have you visit. We don't have facilities for overnight accommodations, but there are several fine hotels within driving distance," he said.

"And do you allow your patients to have guests in the cabins? They're quite large. Ms. Rollings was kind enough to show me one yesterday."

"Actually, we don't allow overnight guests to stay with our patients. You see, we feel it's better for the patient to have some time alone, to be removed from the daily pressures that may have caused them to need a retreat in the first place. Not that that would be the case with you and your Aunt, Karen, but we find that this generally works best for everyone involved."

"So married couples don't stay together in the cabins?"

"No, they don't. Why do you ask?"

"I was just wondering about Max and Dale Almonte. I was with them this week at his father's funeral and Max said he'd been staying here."

"Yes, I see, but I really can't discuss other patients with you. I am sorry, but I know you would appreciate that policy with respect to your Aunt."

"I see. Yes, I quite understand," I said.

"Do you have any written information I could give to my Aunt?" I asked, moving the interview to a conclusion.

"Certainly, we can mail it to you if you'd like."

"No, no. I can easily take the information with me and read it on the plane."

"Well then, let's just go into Ruth's office." He removed a white, eight and a half by eleven, unsealed envelope from a stack of identical envelopes on Ruth's desk. "This will give you all the detailed information and application forms. There are photos there to show your Aunt. We'll be happy to give you any other information you need," he said, handing me the envelope.

"Thank you Doctor Wilson."

"Thank you Karen.   It was a pleasure meeting you," he said, shaking my hand again.

"It was a pleasure meeting you, as well."

And with that, I left Doctor Wilson and made my way out to my car.

Chapter 26

Investment Property

Once in the car, I got out my cell phone and called information for the number for Bard and Strome Commercial Realtors, the office where Dale worked. Information had the number and they connected me "for an additional charge." I resented the charge, but tried to let go of that annoyed feeling. As the phone rang, I hoped the office would be open.

Yea, it was. I asked the receptionist for Dale Almonte and volunteered that Dale was helping me find an investment property. The operator told me what I already knew, that Dale wasn't in the office. I feigned disappointment and asked if there was anyone who could assist me in Dale's absence. Sure enough, one of her associates, Marion Walters, would be happy to meet with me when I arrived. I got directions and estimated my arrival time at ten-thirty.

Traffic was typical LA, four lanes across and bumper to bumper. I kept an eye out for signs as I maneuvered to avoid a collision with an idiot lane weaver. What a jerk! He was going to get wherever two minutes earlier and risk his and everyone else's life to do it. That disproportioned perspective is just so inane. But, that's how road rage starts. I breathed deeply and released the tension I was feeling. Breathe, I rolled down the window and released the bad energy. Better.

I headed north on I-5 and, after forty minutes of cruising and light-listening radio, I was at my exit. The office was located on the twentieth floor of a glass high rise office tower. I found an underground parking lot for the building and left my car with the attendant. I had the elevator to myself as I rode up to the twentieth floor. The elevator opened onto a wood paneled lobby. Glass doors led into the Bard and Strome reception area. There was a directory next to the elevator listing Bard and Strome's offices on three floors of this building. This was a larger firm than I had expected. I entered the office and walked up to a young woman sitting behind a glass desk.

"Hello. Is Marion Walters here? I'm Karen King." I decided to use an alias and figured I'd elevate myself to King. If Dale called in for messages, I didn't want her aware that I was here asking about her. I realized I didn't know if Marion was a man or a woman. The receptionist touched a few buttons on her phone and spoke into the microphone on her headset, "Ms. King here to see you."

"Ms. King, you can have a seat in the lounge. Ms. Walters will be right with you."

Guess "Marion" is actually "Marian" as in Maid Marian. I thanked the receptionist and walked to the leather sofa in the sitting area to her right. This place was looking like a major investment house. The flooring was all light colored hardwood and the white walls were lined with modern lithographs. They were apparently going for that sleek, contemporary look. I expected that the firm was officially closed for the weekend, but there was a moderate level of activity on Saturday morning, nonetheless.

I had just selected a magazine when a young woman in navy slacks and a tan sweater appeared. She was in her early twenties, trim and athletic looking. Shoulder length brown hair framed her thin face.

"Hi. I'm Marian Walters, Dale's assistant," she said.

"Hi," I said, standing and extending my hand. "I'm Karen King. I hear I missed Dale."

"Yes. She had to attend a family funeral," Marian said.

"Sorry to hear that," I said, trying to sound appropriately surprised.

"Is there something I can do for you, Ms. King?" the young woman asked.

"Well, I've been trying to meet with Dale about an investment property in California, for my Aunt. A friend referred me to Dale." Aunt Rose was really coming in handy this week.

"I tried to reach Dale last week, but was told she was out of the office," I said.

"Yes, she was in Chicago at an investment conference," Marian volunteered.

"Dale was in Chicago last week? Where was the conference? I'm from Chicago," I said, the surprise in my voice real this time.

"The conference was last Thursday and Friday, at the Drake. Then she flew back here on Saturday, only to learn she had to fly back for the funeral," Marian said.

"That's a lot of travel for her."

"Part of doing business today," Marian said.

"You know, it's too bad I didn't know Dale was in Chicago. I could have met with her there," I said.

"You probably wouldn't have wanted to meet with her last week. She was really sick. Probably that recycled airplane air. Anyway, she didn't even get to attend most of the conference. She had to spend the time in bed—what a waste. But, you were asking about a real estate investment. Is there something in particular that I can help you with?" Marian said, taking a quick glance at her watch.

"Well, you see a friend recommended me to Dale, and we haven't met yet. So, I thought I'd just take a chance and see if I could meet her, since I was already in LA on another matter. But I'll have to talk with Dale when she's back. I just thought it would be a good chance to meet her and see the office." I was rambling and told myself to slow down.

"Dale will be here mid next week, but I can give you a quick tour of our operation," Marian offered.

"That would be great. I guess I'll miss Dale though. I'm flying out later today. But, I appreciate your taking the time to give me a tour," I said.

As we walked along, I noticed there were private offices along the interior of the floor with secretarial stations just outside them. This arrangement left the floor-to-ceiling windows along the exterior unobstructed, providing a sweeping view of metro LA.

At the end of this side of the floor, we turned the corner. Here, the floor layout changed and there were rooms usurping the view.

"These are our conference rooms along the exterior and private offices along the interior," Marian said. The core of the space is our mailroom. There's an interior stairway that connects our three floors," she added.

As we continued down the hallway, I asked Marian about herself.

"Are you a California native?" I asked.

"Not many of those around," Marian laughed. "No, I'm a Midwestern transplant. Came out to California for school and decided to stay," she said.

We turned the corner once again and this time the exterior wall was lined with private offices.

"These are the partners' offices. All three floors have a similar layout," she offered.

We walked by impressive offices with floor to ceiling windows overlooking the city. I caught a glimpse of oriental carpets and leather sofas as we walked by these empty rooms. Apparently the partners didn't work on Saturdays. We turned the corner again and we were heading back to the reception area.

"Well, thank you for my tour, Marian," I said and extended my hand once again.

"You're very welcome. And if I can be of any help with your investments, just let me know. Here's my card."

She handed me her business card which listed her title as a sales associate. I imagined she worked on some form of commission and I felt a little guilty taking her time to give me a tour. But just a little and it passed in a moment.

Waiting for the elevator, I thought about Dale's being in Chicago Friday evening. That gave her opportunity and she certainly had motive. Her husband would be inheriting a fortune. Finally, I was getting somewhere. I thought about getting into Dale and Max's house and doing some exploring, but, just by establishing her presence in Chicago, I'd found enough to get the police looking in another direction. I didn't want to break any more laws than I had to. And, if I was caught breaking into their place out here, I'd really be sunk. I figured Max and Dale were likely to have an alarm system in place. Maybe I was just talking myself out of it, but it seemed to me I should take what I'd learned and head home. Head home right after visiting the gallery that is.

Chapter
27

The Gallery

10000 Wilshire was only a mile from the Bard and Strome office. The thought of finding parking in LA again didn't thrill me. But no one walks in downtown LA and flagging taxis is impossible. It's a city of drivers and I joined the ranks, moving my rented mobile the mile down Wilshire. It wouldn't be quick getting in and out of the lots, but it would probably be faster than walking the mile there and back. Just, as it turned out. I finally found parking under the building next to the building in which the gallery was located. Why do they hide the parking lots like that?

The gallery was on the second floor of the Trellisse Building. The lobby was travertine with escalators leading up to the mezzanine level, where shops and restaurants were located. Banks of elevators flanked the escalators, but I chose to walk up the moving stairway. A second bank of escalators carried me above the restaurant level to a more exclusive shopping floor where Armani, Gucci, and Cartier boutiques displayed the latest greatest. The Otillier Gallery was across from Armani, just to the right of the escalator, as I stepped off. Four Rembrandt etchings were displayed on easels in the exterior window and the words *"Marshall Otillier Gallery"* were lettered in gold on a persimmon wall behind these master works. I pulled open the heavy glass doors and was greeted by a young woman in a long straight black dress.

"Hi, I'm Karen Prince. I believe Andre is expecting me."

"Oh, welcome. Yes, he asked me to call him as soon as you arrived. Just one moment and I'll tell him you're here," she said.

I entertained myself looking at four more etchings on the walls of this anteroom while the young lady went to her desk to call Andre.

In a few minutes, Andre came through the interior set of glass doors and welcomed me with a hug. We'd worked together on my show here years ago and I had consulted for him on a Ruysch and a Bossecart work in the intervening years.

"Welcome! Your painting arrived yesterday afternoon. I have it all uncrated and waiting for you in my office. Come in, come in."

And with that, Andre pressed a code into the key pad to the right of the interior glass doors which slowly swung open. I followed Andre to the interior of the gallery, past works any museum would envy, to Andre's well appointed office. There, on the dark brown leather sofa, sat my painting. I went to it and lifted it. The frame was heavy carved wood I'd not seen before. But the work—yes, this was my work. I carried it to the light on his desk and looked for my signature. Not there.

"Andre, can I borrow your magnifying glass?"

"Certainly," he said and handed me the silver handled glass from his top desk drawer.

"And let me adjust the lights for you," he said, turning up the rheostat.

"Yes, better. Thanks, Andre." I held the magnifying glass over the edge of the table in the painting. The paint was slightly thicker in the area of the painting where I had signed the piece. I looked closely at the flowers and remembered the orange lily I'd studied so closely to get the veining just right. Yes, this was my piece. I had worked for weeks on this piece and had finally gotten the light on the flowers to my satisfaction. I'd sold it through a gallery in Chicago which was no longer in existence.   Its owner had retired and moved to warmer climes.

"Yes, Andre, this is definitely my piece. I don't know how much Marshall shared with you about the story behind this—"

"The Morgan's auction find!" he said, letting me know that Marshall had shared the story with him.

"Yes— A shame for them I suppose," I said.

"Well, they have a beautiful, masterful work," Andre said. "And they know it or they wouldn't have bought it. It's a gorgeous piece, even if the artist isn't dead," he said teasingly.

I laughed at his comment and the absurdity of the fact that paintings increase in value with the death of the painter.

"Let's call Marshall, shall we?"

"By all means," Andre said and extended the desk phone to me.

I set my work back on the sofa and took the phone from Andre. Marshall was at his New York gallery and wasn't surprised by the confirmation of my first opinion.

"Just wanted to be sure—before I gave the news to the Morgans, darling. Thank you for taking the time and making the trip to the gallery."

"Not at all. But Marshall, would you mind if I took this painting home with me to study it more closely? I'd like a chance to look at it in my studio. You can ask the Morgans if they'd like me to remove the paint over my signature. I can restore it for them if they'd like."

"That's an excellent idea, my dear. They know your work and I'm sure they'll be happy to have a signed Prince. I'll talk to them and get back to you, but do take the painting with you if you'd like. You can ship it back to me in a week or so. I'll let them know you'll be doing the conservation work on their piece."

"Thanks, Marshall. I'll give you back to Andre."

With that, Marshall authorized Andre to pack the painting for me and I left with my old friend wrapped in glassine, bubble wrap, and a protective carton. Andre gave me a roll of tape to use in repacking the piece after the airport inspections which would undoubtedly follow. But it would be worth the hassle to have the painting home for a week or so.

And head home was just what I did. The trip back consisted of the same series of herding and waiting, jostling and lugging, complicated a bit by the painting, which I balanced on top of my roll-on luggage. I made my scheduled flight, the five-twelve out of LAX, with time to spare.

For all of the inconvenience, there was a moment on the flight when the miracle of being at thirty thousand feet hit me. We were above the clouds and the pinks and oranges of the sunset tinted the sky. The world seemed momentarily peaceful. I closed my eyes and even managed to doze without either getting a crook in my neck or jerking myself awake as my head fell forward.

Four real hours and a two hour time change later, we landed at O'Hare and I called my limo. It was eleven-thirty Saturday night and O'Hare was in one of its quieter states. I rolled my luggage past closed newsstands and sandwich vendors. The smell of popcorn still lingered in the air around the now abandoned red popcorn carts.

I took the escalator to the lower level and the brisk night air chilled me as I exited the terminal. A few taxis stood in line and I crossed the first street to the central median for driver pickup. A black limo was waiting for me. I waved to the driver and he got out of the car and placed my luggage in the trunk. I settled in the back seat with my *"Butterfly Bouquet"* and thought of Mark. Hopefully he wouldn't be too soundly asleep when I got home.

Chapter 28

Richard's Confession

Sunday morning we slept until eight, which was a real luxury. We put in our time on the lakefront jogging path and picked up fresh fruit and eggs from the little grocery in Mark's building on our way home.

After breakfast, I called Richard Fox at home. I knew he was the one who'd been in Martin Thomas's office and he knew I knew. I had a theory about who'd killed George and it wasn't Richard. But he had committed a crime and I needed to know how that fit in with this picture. Somewhat surprisingly, Fox agreed to meet with me and invited me to his place. Even though I didn't think he'd killed George, I didn't want to be alone with him on his ground. I asked him to come to Mark's. He hesitated, but I knew he was motivated to meet with me and I held my ground. He finally agreed to come over in an hour.

Richard Fox was dressed in a Gucci trench coat, cashmere sweater, and black tailored slacks. He was the picture of the sophisticated city gentleman. To look at him, you'd never guess he'd been busy breaking and entering and conking another lawyer on the head this week.

"Come in," I said. I felt like the spider talking to the fly. Mark had insisted on staying in the bedroom while I met with Richard. Although I didn't expect Richard to attack me, I felt somewhat comforted knowing that Mark was there.

Richard came in and we sat across from each other at the dining room table.

"Jane convinced me to meet with you," he said without preamble. "I told her everything when I got back to the office after you saw me at Martin Thomas's office."

We looked into each other's eyes. I didn't know what to say and he continued.

"I hadn't intended to hit Martin. I just wanted to scare him. All his book would do is bring up old topics that were better left buried. I didn't want to put Marge through all that again."

I nodded but I didn't say anything. I didn't want to interrupt his flow.

"I'd met with him a month ago. I tried to get him to see he wasn't going to make a fortune with this book like he dreamed. It'd only serve to rehash old news and embarrass me in front of my friends and family. I was desperate and Thomas just laughed at me. He said that wasn't his concern," Fox said.

"So last week, I thought I'd just give him a scare and maybe he'd stop. I figured I'd take his files and make it hard for him to write about me. I studied his work patterns and I knew he came into the office early, before his staff. So I waited in the hallway outside his office until he got there. I gave him a few minutes to get settled at his desk and then I let myself in. I tried to reason with him, but he just wouldn't budge. I shoved him and he shoved back and we ended up in a fight. I'd brought my gun just to scare him. I pulled it out and made him sit back down at his desk. I was crazy with anger and I knocked him on the head. I was looking for the files when you came in. And that's the story."

"Have you told this to the police?" I asked.

"No. I'm going to meet with Martin and see if I can't make some kind of settlement with him. I lost my head but maybe I can make it right. He wants money and I want the story to die. I think we can work something out. Jane made me see that. I should have seen this myself before, but maybe it's not too late," he said.

"Maybe," I said. "And what about George?"

"George? What do you mean?" he said, sounding genuinely surprised.

"What was George's role in all of this?" I asked.

"George. My good old partner George. He certainly was a wretch. I'm glad he's dead, but I didn't kill him," Richard said. And, somehow, I believed him.

"Who do you think did kill George?" I asked.

"Maybe someone else he was blackmailing," Richard said.

"You're saying George was blackmailing you?" I repeated.

"Yes, for many years. And the kicker was he didn't need the money. He just liked the power he held over me. He was sick." Disdain distorted Richard's face.

"So that's why he changed his testimony during your trial?" I asked.

"Yes, he figured he'd be better off with a partner who wasn't convicted and whom he had in his pocket," Richard said.

"I went along with it for fifteen long years, but I just couldn't take it anymore. Anytime we disagreed on a business deal he'd use what he held over my head to get his way. I called his bluff seven years ago and told him to take a flying leap. Turns out I should have done that from the start. He just walked away. When it wasn't easy for him anymore, it wasn't fun," Richard said.

"So that's when you sold your property in the country and ended your partnership with George," I said.

"That's it. So, you see, I didn't have any reason to kill him. He wasn't threatening me anymore. I don't know who he was tormenting, but it wasn't me," Richard said.

"Thanks for telling me all this Richard."

"Are you going to tell all this to the police?" he asked.

"I don't see what purpose that would serve. I don't think you killed George, so I don't think I'd be withholding evidence. My interest is in finding out who the murderer is, so the police don't hold Alice responsible," I said.

"I appreciate that," he said quietly.

"So this will just be between us, as far as I'm concerned. But you do need to make it right with Martin Thomas."

"I'll do that. Thank you. And good luck with Alice," he said.

And with that Richard left the apartment.

Chapter 29

The Stable

Mark came out of the bedroom when he heard the front door close. "Well, do you believe him?" Mark asked.

"Oddly enough, I do. It's a crazy story, but I think he's telling me the truth."

"So what's your next move, Sherlock?"

"I'm going to trace George's steps on his last day. I have a feeling the answer is there waiting for me," I said.

"So where will you start?"

"At the stable. Darlene said George was supposed to be out riding on Friday. Let's see if he ever showed up at the stable."

"Want some company? I'm not going into the office today."

"By all means, Watson," I said, smiling at him.

I called Polly and got the name and address of the stable where George kept his horse. It was the only stable in the city, just west of Lincoln Park.

Before we left, I unwrapped my old friend and looked for a place to temporarily hang "Butterfly Bouquet." I removed a painting from the living room wall and hung my painting in its place. As Mark drove us to the stable, I filled him in on the painting's story.

We were there in fifteen minutes and we parked in the lot behind an old red barn. It was hard to imagine that when this barn had been built it was in harmony with its neighborhood. Now it was an anachronism, one that had caused a huge political battle twenty years ago when the owners restored it to its current function. But the horse folks used their money and power and won an exemption for having horses in the city. The parking lot was filled with Beemers and Mercedes. It looked like a lot of people were riding today.

It was close to noon as we walked into the stable. There was a group of women in riding gear standing near the entrance. They stopped their conversation and looked at us as we walked in. This was evidently a closed circle and newcomers were noticed.

"Can I help you?" A woman in her fifties broke from the group and walked towards us. Her stiff manner told me she hadn't yet decided whether we were welcome. She was thin and had her dark hair pulled back, rather like a horse's tail.

"We're looking for riding friends of George Almonte," I said, holding out my hand. "I'm Karen Prince and this is my friend, Mark Jordan."

"Elaine Holt," the woman said, shaking my hand. She had a firm grip and piercing dark eyes. "I remember you from the service. I didn't get a chance to talk to you at Darlene's," she said.

"Yes, I couldn't stay long. Actually, it's George's death that brings me here today."

She paused, then said, "We're all still in shock about his murder."

"Yes, I am too. And I'm trying to understand exactly what happened to him. Would you mind if I asked you a few questions about George?"

"Here, come into my office so we can be more comfortable and talk in private," Elaine said and walked toward a small office to the right of the entry door. She sat down behind an old oak desk and Mark and I sat in the two wooden chairs in front of it.

"So, what would you like to know?" Elaine asked.

"Do you by any chance know if George was here on Friday, the day he was killed?" I asked.

"Yes, I know for a fact that he was. We were all here. We were getting ready for this afternoon's show."

"Were you here the whole time that George was?" I asked.

"I'm here all day every day," she said with a smile. "This is my life—this stable, the horses, and the riders."

"Did George seem anxious or concerned about anything that day?" I asked.

"He was excited about the show, like everybody here. And we were all working on our routines. So people were sort of high strung that day. But I don't think he was upset," Elaine said.

"Was anyone with him?"

"No, Darlene never came to the stable. I think she was afraid of horses. He would have liked her to ride, but, you know, it's either in your blood or it's not. She just wasn't into horses."

"Was he late or did he leave early?" I asked, fishing for something out of the ordinary.

"I don't remember him being late and I know he didn't leave early, but one thing was strange. He got a call while he was riding. I remember, because we were in the middle of a routine and he stopped to try to answer his phone. It's against our policy to have a cell phone turned on here in the stable. We don't need that kind of distraction."

"So who called him?"

"Well, I don't know. But I think he must have been expecting a call to have had the phone on. Like I said, our riders aren't supposed to do that," Elaine said.

"So what did he do when the phone rang?"

"Well, he fished around for his phone and tried to stay on the horse at the same time. I think he missed the call. But I remember he got off the horse and went outside with his phone."

"Do you think he called whoever it was back?"

"Well, I don't know for sure, I didn't follow him, but that's what I thought he was going to do," Elaine said.

"Did he come back in after that?"

"Yes, he came back in and finished riding. We were almost done for the day anyway."

"Did George drive back home with anyone, do you know?" Mark asked.

"George usually took a taxi to and from the stable. He hated driving in the city," Elaine said.

"Interesting. Elaine, would you mind if we ask the group out there if they talked to George that day or saw him leave?" I asked.

"Sure, be my guest," she said, getting up from her chair. We all rose, and Mark and I thanked Elaine for her time and help.

We walked out to the group of riders. There were six women and three men, all in full riding gear. They stood talking, waiting for Elaine's return. The horses were walking around in the fenced riding area. I could see stalls and hear other horses at the far end of the arena.

Elaine introduced us to the group and told them we wanted to talk to them about George. I asked the group in general if they had been at the stable with George the Friday he was killed. Everyone nodded, except one of the men who said he'd been ill and hadn't come out to the stable that day.

"Did George seem nervous or upset to any of you?" I asked. People looked at each other and shook their heads no. There was a general consensus that he hadn't seemed any different that day. No one had seen anyone else with him. No one had seen him get into a taxi. This wasn't proving to be very informative and I knew the group interview wasn't the most productive format. I gave each of them one of my cards and asked them to call me if they thought of anything that might be helpful.

"Any little thing you remember might help in finding out what really happened to George," I said. "I'm certain Alice was not responsible for George's death," I added. I didn't think any of these folks were friends of Alice's since she didn't ride in the city. But still, I figured they wouldn't want her to be blamed for George's death if she wasn't responsible for it.

We said our goodbyes and as we were walking to our car, one of the women came running after us.

"Hey," she called.

"I'm Rachel," she said. "This is probably nothing, but you know, you mentioned George taking a taxi. Well, it just struck me—he didn't take a taxi that day."

"He didn't?" Mark and I said simultaneously.

"No, I saw him get into his car," Rachel said.

"You're saying he drove?" I said.

"Actually, someone else was driving. A young blonde fellow," Rachel said.

"A young blonde fellow? Are you sure?"

"I had to get a new blanket from my car. And I saw George get in the car with, well, I think it was his son. Max's been out here once or twice before."

"Did you talk to him?" I asked.

"No. My car was on the far side of the lot and George seemed to be in a hurry to leave. He had the stable folks brush down Ranger, which he usually does himself. So, I didn't want to interrupt him.

Anyway, I was just going out to the car when I saw George getting into the passenger side of the car and then they pulled out of the parking lot. Probably nothing, but I thought I'd mention it."

"Thanks, Rachel. Would you mind giving me your phone number in case we have to reach you later? It may be more important than you realize."

"Oh, no problem. Here, let me jot it down for you," she said.

"Have the police been out here to talk to you all?" Mark asked.

"No. No one here's heard from them," she said.

"Thanks. This is very helpful," I said. We shook hands and Rachel went back into the building.

As we drove out of the stable parking lot Mark said, "I thought Max was in California that day."

"He was, according to Max and the staff at the Beachfront," I said.

Chapter 30

A Meeting

Mark drove us back to his place, taking the side streets east to Lakeshore Drive. I excitedly sketched out my idea about George's murder for him and watched his expression, as much as I could from the passenger's seat. He thought it was possible, but I could tell he wasn't convinced. As we talked about it, the idea of a meeting with everyone involved came to me. I got out my cell phone as we turned onto Lakeshore Drive. I dialed Frank's number and watched the joggers and the bicyclists along the lakefront as I waited for the phone to ring through. Frank answered on the third ring.

"Frank, glad I got you at home. Do you think you can convince the State's Attorney and Cavanaugh to have a meeting with us tomorrow afternoon?" I asked. "I have an idea that I think will turn the investigation in a completely new direction—away from Alice," I added to encourage him to say "yes."

"Well, it's a bit of late notice, but I should think if we're willing to go out to them, they'd take an hour to meet with us, given the gravity of the case."

"Well, actually, it would be better if they could come in here, to the city I mean. I want to have Max, Darlene, Dale, and David, all there as well. And Alice, of course," I said.

"Well, that's a tall order," I could hear the hesitation in Frank's voice.

"Yes, I know. But I think I have an idea they haven't considered about who killed George. And time is so important. In a few days, Max and Dale will be back in California. And then it will be harder than ever to get them here," I said.

"I'll give it my best shot, Karen. That's all I can promise," Frank said.

"That's all I'm asking. Thanks, Frank. I think this is really important," I said. "We'll be back at Mark's in a few minutes. Give us a call there when you've reached the State's Attorney."

"I'll call you back as soon as I know something," Frank said and rang off.

Then I called Alice and told her about my idea for a meeting. I asked her to be ready to head in here tomorrow morning if Frank succeeded in setting up the meeting.

"I'll ask Louise and Tony to drive you," I said, concerned about her strength.

"No, no, I'll drive myself. I'll be fine," she said.

Frank called back as we were finishing dinner at Mark's.

"It's all set," he said.

"Really! That's great," I said.

"We're meeting them at my office, tomorrow afternoon at two. The State's Attorney wants to interview Max, Dale, Darlene, and David, anyway, before the trial. Cavanaugh's already talked to them all, but the State's Attorney hasn't yet. He was planning to go into Chicago sometime this week to meet with them, so he's setting it up for tomorrow," Frank said.

"Oh Frank, that's perfect," I said. "I'll call Alice and let her know the time for the meeting."

So Monday afternoon found Darlene and David, Max and Dale, Mark and me, Alice, Frank, Detective Cavanaugh and Milt Freedman, the State's Attorney, gathered in a conference room in Frank's office. Frank had one of his young associates at the meeting as well, taking notes. We'd talked with Milt Freedman before the meeting, and convinced him to let me talk to the group before he started his interviews. I told him I was sure I'd have him convinced Alice wasn't the killer if he'd just give me ten minutes in the room with this group. So, Frank opened the meeting with a few words, and then turned the meeting over to me.

I stood up, looked at everyone around the table, and said, "We're all here because someone in this room killed George Almonte. So far, the investigation's been directed at Alice. But I'm going to show that quite a number of other people here could have killed him—and had the motive—and opportunity to do it."

Each person looked at the others sitting around the table. Max rolled his eyeballs to the ceiling, pushed his chair back, and sighed out loud.

"I don't know why I even agreed to come here," Max said, getting up out of his chair and looking at me with contempt. "Come on, Dale, let's get out of here."

"Sit down," boomed Milt Freedman. Milt was a good six foot four with a deep baritone voice that got your attention. "Remember, you're meeting with me in a few minutes and I want to hear what she has to say. You can too."

There was a knock on the door and a tall man in his late thirties, wearing a dark sweater and pants, entered the room.

"Please come in," I said, rising from my seat. "This is Mr. Temple, from the medical examiner's office," I said, introducing him to the rest of the gathering. "Last week Mr. Temple performed certain medical tests on George's blood. As a part of those tests, I suggested that he compare a sample of George's blood with the blood tests performed on Alice when she was admitted to the hospital. Mr. Temple is here to tell us the results of those tests. Mr. Temple, can you tell us what you found?"

"Yes, I can. Both Alice and George had diazepam, a prescription non-barbiturate, sedative-hypnotic drug, commonly known as Valium, in their systems. George had enough to knock him out. Alice had more—enough to kill her."

Max jumped up saying, "So that proves that Alice had the drug and gave it to George and then tried to kill herself." His voice was agitated and his face flushed red.

Dale grabbed Max's arm. "Quiet, Max. Sit down," she said, giving him a menacing look and pulling him back into his seat. Max glared back at her.

"Actually, it doesn't prove any such thing," I said. "It introduces the possibility—that someone with access to this particular barbiturate—administered it to both Alice and George. The question then becomes, who had access to this drug?" Looking at each person as I mentioned them, I said, "Maybe Darlene had a prescription? Or, perhaps Dale stole the drug from the pharmacy at the Beachfront? Or Max, maybe you got a prescription from the doctor while you were at the Beachfront."

"This is ridiculous speculation!" Max shouted. "I don't see why I should stay here and listen to this."

"Perhaps you were the one who gave the drug to your father, then drove him out to Alice's. You left him there by the pond knowing the police would think Alice had killed him. You hit him over the head with Alice's fire iron and put it in the barn for the police to find," I said.

"That's ridiculous. I was in California and you know it."

"I don't know any such thing. In fact, quite the contrary—I believe you were in Chicago." I had everyone's attention now. "I think you traded places with Dale on Wednesday at the Beachfront. It was easy enough to do. She came to visit you and you left in her place. That's why you said you were ill, so you could stay in your cabin and avoid contact with any of the other patients or staff. You left in Dale's clothes and then flew to Chicago dressed as Dale. She already had her ticket and hotel room because she was supposed to attend a conference. I'll bet if we check, we'll find she didn't attend any of the meetings. It was easy enough to pass for her at the airport, the car rental, and the hotel. Even if they thought you were cross dressing, hey, what were they going to say? It would have been none of their business. You had her identification and the two of you look enough alike to pass for one another on a driver's license photo."

"That's utter nonsense. Alice did it and then tried to kill herself!" Now Dale was shouting.

"No, she didn't," I said, as calmly and firmly as I could. "Max, you drove out to Alice's house again on Tuesday night and slipped in the back way. Everyone in the county knows where she keeps the key. I'm sure you knew too, from the times you visited Alice and your father out there over the years," I said. He was shaking his head. The room was dead silent. Everyone around the table looked at Max and then at me.

"You put the drug in Alice's glass of wine. She never knew what hit her. When she was passed out, you arranged the scene to look like a suicide," I said.

"If Louise hadn't come by when she did, your little plan would have worked. Alice would have been dead. I would have been crushed and probably stopped asking any questions. That would have been the end of it."

Now both Max and Dale leapt from their chairs. They stormed for the door. Max yelled, "We're out of here."

153

Detective Cavanaugh sprang up after them. They were in the corridor.

I heard Detective Cavanaugh yell, "Stop right there."

I ran to the doorway and saw Cavanaugh had his gun drawn. A secretary walking down the hall with an armful of files screamed and ran into an open office. Two other people from Frank's firm were pressed against the walls, too frightened to move. Frank ran to the phone and instructed the receptionist to lock the front door. Freedman ran out the other conference room door after Cavanaugh.

I ran back into the conference room, over to Alice and gave her a hug.

Detective Cavanaugh had Max and Dale in handcuffs in the lobby by the time the rest of us got there.

"I owe you a thank you, Karen," Cavanaugh said. "It looks like we had the wrong person after all."

"It looks like it," I agreed. "At least this gives you an alternative theory to look into. But you know, it could have been one of the other people in the room as well," I said, looking him in the eye. I didn't have a chance to talk about David or Darlene yet."

"Well, no one else ran out of there. I think we have our murderers now," Detective Cavanaugh said as he escorted Max and Dale from the building.

Chapter 31

Pond Scum

Alice, Donald, Mark and I had spent the evening in Chicago celebrating Alice's demotion from prime suspect. Hopefully, life would get back on its normal track now. Alice and I'd agreed to meet at her country place at noon today for our annual end of the season ritual: pulling the floating raft from her pond. Driving back home this morning, the traffic was heavy until Elgin and then it was open road. I made it home in three and a half hours, which gave me an hour before I had to be at Alice's.

Truffles greeted me with a trill and an ankle rub. It looked like she wasn't holding a grudge against me for my prolonged absence. I rubbed her kitty-head and gave her a can of her special treat. Louise had stacked the mail on the kitchen table and I groaned mentally when I saw the heap covering a full three square feet. Most of it would be catalogues, but it would still take me hours to get through it all. I put that out of my mind and went on to more fun things.

I brought my painting in from the car and carried it up to my studio. There, I carefully unwrapped the packing material once again and rolled up the glassine for future use. You wouldn't believe how expensive this art wax paper is. Then I carefully spread out a pad and lay a lint free sheet over it. I turned the painting face side down and studied the back of the frame. Hand hewn wooden pegs held the painting in place in the frame. Someone had gone to great lengths to make this piece look seventeenth century. I remove the pegs with needle nose pliers, being careful not to put too much pressure on the pegs. They came out rather easily, which confirmed that they hadn't been in place all that long. The painting seemed to be undamaged on the edges and on the surface, other than the repainting of the lower right hand section to hide my signature. When I removed the painting, I noticed a slight change in the grain of the wood on the back of the frame. Usually these frames were carved from a solid piece of wood, so this change intrigued me. Looking closely with a magnifying glass, I saw an edge to the piece which had been inserted into the right panel on the back of the frame. I felt a slight tingling sensation on my forehead, about an inch above the bridge of my nose. This sounds strange, but it's happened before. It comes at times of realizations, signaling a new awareness. I knew I needed to look at this more closely.

I brought a spotlight over and examined every inch of the frame. Along the interior side of the rabbit, the area inside the frame on which the painting rests, I found a small metal pin. While pressing this pin, I pushed first up, then down on the patched area on the back of the frame. A slight movement, at first, and then the three inch panel slid down and back, under the adjacent piece of the frame. I gasped.

There was a small chamber built into the frame, much like a secret drawer in a desk. Inside the chamber was a small leather pouch. I used my tweezers and pulled the pouch from its long sealed hiding place. With shaking hands, I untied the drawstrings. I could see fabric inside the pouch, but its weight in the palm of my hand told me there was something wrapped in the fabric. Carefully I removed and unrolled the linen—a gold necklace and ring shone in daylight for the first time in perhaps hundreds of years.

I recognized the design of the jewelry from the portraits I had studied at the Rijksmuseum—it was seventeenth century Dutch. I needed to share this with someone and called Marshall on his cell phone number.

"Marshall, Karen—I have news for you and the Morgans. You know that period frame the Morgans bought with my painting—well, it has a secret compartment—and I just found a period necklace and ring hidden in the frame! I haven't had anyone look at it, of course, but I think this is the real thing!"

"Oh my heavens. You know, everything that fellow touches turns to gold— now you have literally proved it!"

I laughed, a nervous release of energy. "It's incredibly beautiful— I can't wait for you to see it."

"I spoke with the auction house this morning. After you called me from the gallery, I wanted to press them for whatever information they would give me on the seller of the painting. The manager of the auction house said the seller was about twenty-four years old,

American, and said he was traveling the world for a year after he settled his uncle's estate in London. That's why the auction house bought the painting from the young man, instead of just taking it on consignment. The manager said they were comfortable they could get ten thousand pounds from the sale of the piece, regardless of attribution, based on the quality of the work. When I told the manager that you were the artist, he said they'd like to see more of your paintings. I'm sure the Morgans will want to see more as well."

"Well, that's very flattering and great news. Do you know what they paid for the painting?" I asked.

"Twenty thousand pounds. They'll certainly more than double that in the value of the jewelry you found."

"I'm sure they will. These pieces are exquisite."

"Karen, I have to call them right now and give them the good news. You are magnificent, my dear!"

I smiled as I hung up and replaced the painting in the frame. I hung the painting in my bedroom where I could look at it regularly for the short time it would be with me. The jewelry I tried on, admired it in the mirror, and then placed it in my own secret hiding place—the ice tray in my freezer. I never use ice.

I made a quick change into my garden work jeans and drove over to Alice's. This would be a messy job, so I took the Jeep instead of the Boxster. It was just noon as I pulled into her lane and drove up to the pond. Most of the trees had shed their leaves and the sky was a steely gray. I hoped we'd get the darn raft out of the pond before it started to rain. We'd agreed to meet at the pond, but I didn't see any sign of Alice or the tractor she would use to pull out the raft.

I parked the Jeep in the pull-through in front of the barn and walked to the edge of the pond. I looked at the water and thought of the changes that had taken place in our lives since Alice and I had met out here. Marriage had dissolved into tears and anger for Alice. My career, as well as my fortunes, had changed dramatically. As I wondered about the unexpected twists in life's road, my eye caught sight of a deflated ball bobbing along the shore line. I walked closer, trying not to sink into the marshy fringe of the pond. The water was only six inches deep at this end and the rains made the shoreline soft and mucky. I needed a stick to reach the ball. Looking around, my eye settled on the fall burn pile. I jogged over to it and disentangled a five foot long branch. Now armed with my retrieval stick, I jogged back the hundred feet to the pond and tip-toed as close to the pond edge as I could without sinking into the mire. The ball was wedged in some marsh grass, about three feet off the shoreline. Stretching, I was able to drag it out of the water.

On closer inspection, it turned out not to be a ball at all. It was a mask—a mask of Max. There was a bit of rope still around it. Someone had sunk this mask of Max. They'd probably tied it around a stone and thrown it into the pond.

My head reeled. Had it been Max that picked up his father at the riding stable and brought him out here to kill him—or was it someone wearing this mask? Yesterday, we'd all concluded that Max killed George. In running from the room he seemed to confirm his guilt. But Max had never admitted to the murder. In fact, he swore his innocence to Cavanaugh and the State's Attorney. What was this mask of Max doing in the pond? Had we jumped to the wrong conclusion? Had Cavanaugh been right, all along?

I heard a car coming up the lane. It had to be Alice—and she'd be here in a few minutes. Quickly, I tossed the mask back to the edge of the pond.

I needed to hide. I wanted to see what Alice would do when she saw the mask. But what to do with my car? I pulled the Jeep out of sight around the side of the barn, killed the engine, and ducked in the back door of the barn. I stood there for a minute as my eyes adjusted to the darkness. Then I crouched beneath the window overlooking the pond, raising my head just high enough to peer out. I felt awful spying on my friend, but I had to know—to dispel my doubt.

I watched Alice pull up and park in the same spot I'd just had the Jeep.

She got out and walked to the pond, looking around. She was probably wondering if I'd been there yet. Then she must have seen it. She looked over her shoulder again. Looking around her—for what? For me? Were my foot prints there in the muddy edge of the pond? No—she grabbed the stick I'd discarded and pulled the mask toward her. She lifted it with the stick—she held it in her hand. Then she placed it on the shore and ran towards me.

I moved to the back of the barn, behind the tractor. Then I thought Alice might come for the tractor and I looked for another place to hide. I saw the large riding lawn mower and tucked myself into a ball in the corner behind it. I didn't think she'd see me there, at least at first glance. I felt a fool, crouched there, confused, frightened that Alice might indeed have killed George. I waited what seemed like an eternity. It was probably about four minutes. She should have been here by now. Then it struck me, what if she didn't come here? She could have gone to the stable. She could have run up to the house to phone Cavanaugh. But, she would have used her cell phone if she wanted to make a call. She surely had it in the car with her. I made my way back to the window, ready to run to my hiding place at the first sound. But no sound came. Alice reappeared with a black garbage bag.

She must have gone to the stable. Of course. She used the stable regularly. The barn was rarely used this time of year.

Alice walked back to the edge of the pond. She put the mask into the bag.

As if the curtain had lifted on a theater stage, I saw Alice in my mind's eye telephoning George on his last Friday afternoon at the Chicago stable. She could have arranged to meet him after his ride, to pick him up, to talk. That was the phone call. Then suppose she wore the mask while she waited in the lot. Probably told George it was a joke, a present for Max perhaps. They laughed. She gave him a cup of coffee, a cup laced with Valium. That's what the medical examiner had found in his blood—not enough to kill him, just enough to knock him out.

She drove straight to the country with George passed out on the seat next to her. Once at her house she went into the kitchen and grabbed the fire iron. She drove to the pond and pushed him out of the car. He started coming to and she struck him on the back of the head with the poker. She panicked and hid it in the barn. I tried to think of a way it could have been an accident. But the mask, the drugs, it all was premeditated. The divorce, and then his recent calls, had been too much for her.

The movie in my mind ended and I focused on the actual scene in front of me through the barn window. Alice was getting into her car with the black bag. I had to stop her before she destroyed the evidence. I should have called Detective Cavanaugh from the car, but I jumped into my Jeep, instead, and followed her up to the house. I wanted to hear the story from Alice herself. Her car was in the turn around circle. I pulled up next to her on the lawn. I didn't want my car blocked behind hers. I walked up to the house and looked in through the window. Alice sat at the table with the black bag in front of her. She stared into space. I let myself in the kitchen door.

Alice, are you all right?" I asked.

She looked up at me and shook her head. "No. No I'm not," she said in a weak, faltering voice.

I pointed to the bag and asked, "Alice, what is that?"

"I don't know," Alice said feebly. "It's from the pond."

She didn't seem to be hiding it from me. Maybe she was as stunned as I was. A glimmer of hope rose in my heart.

"Can I look in the bag?"

"Go ahead," she said. Then, added, "Wait, don't touch it. Just open the bag and look in."

I opened the bag.

"What is it Alice?" I asked again.

"It's a mask—a mask of Max—someone must have worn it. George's killer must have worn it. Karen, this must mean Max didn't kill George after all! I thought this whole awful thing was over! Now—now the police will think I killed George. They'll be after me again—"

Relief flooded through every pore of my being. Why had I doubted my friend? "We'll figure this out," I said.

"Why would the killer have worn a mask?" Alice asked.

"I figure the killer must have worn it when he—or she—picked up George at the Chicago riding stable. The mask would have hidden the killer's face while waiting in the car for George," I said.

"The mask certainly wouldn't have fooled George, but from a distance, from outside the car, it would have looked like Max," Alice said.

"There may be some clue on the mask—maybe DNA from the person who wore it," I said, more hopeful than I'd felt since I first saw the mask.

"But it's been in the pond for over a week now. Wouldn't any evidence have been washed away?" Alice asked.

"I don't know for sure, but maybe not. It'll have to be tested."

We both realized with that comment what we had to do next. We had to call Detective Cavanaugh, once again.

Alice made the call. It would be in her favor if she called the police and turned in the mask herself. But Detective Cavanaugh wasn't in his office. The receptionist didn't know when he'd be back, and suggested we leave a message on his voice mail. Alice told her it was urgent and the receptionist said she'd try to reach him after she transferred Alice to the detective's voice mail.

There was a pause while Alice waited for Cavanaugh's voice mail message to end. She looked at me as she said, "Detective Cavanaugh, it's Alice Almonte—We found something in the pond that you should see—Karen and I are here now. We think it has to do with George's murder. It's a mask—a mask of Max Almonte." She paused and then continued, "Please call me as soon as you can. You'd better come out here right away. We'll be here. Just come out here as soon as you get this," she said and hung up the phone.

"I hope he gets this message soon," Alice said.

"So do I—I thought this was all over yesterday afternoon."

While we waited for Cavanaugh to call, I confessed to Alice about finding the mask and hiding in the barn. I felt awful to have doubted her, but I would have felt worse with that between us.

"I understand—everything is so crazy right now," Alice said. We hugged, reassuring each other of our friendship.

As we sat there waiting for Cavanaugh's call, an idea took shape in my mind. "Alice, tell me something—if it wasn't Max and Dale who killed George, who do you think it was?"

"There's no doubt in my mind—Darlene must have done it," Alice said.

"I think so too. It's the only thing that makes sense now. And she had the most to gain."

"So, what do we do?" Alice asked.

"I have an idea," I said.

And I laid out my plan.

161

Chapter 32

The Sting

Alice dialed Darlene's number on the kitchen phone. I listened in on the living room extension.

"Hello," Darlene said.

"Darlene, this is Alice Almonte."

Dead silence.

"Darlene, can you hear me?"

She paused before answering, "Yes, I can hear you all right. What do you want?"

"I have something of yours here. Something I think you'll want to purchase from me," Alice said cryptically.

"What are you talking about?" Darlene said in an annoyed tone.

"I'm talking about a little rubber mask of Max—you know what I mean—it's the mask you threw in the pond—it washed up on shore today," Alice said in a taunting tone.

There was more silence from Darlene. Then she said, "What are you going to do with it?"

"I thought I'd sell it to you, Darlene—I'd rather get back some of what I lost in the divorce than see you in jail. So I'm offering to sell it to you. But you have to come up here today, this afternoon, or else I'm going to give this to Detective Cavanaugh. And Darlene—bring your check book—I want the money market fund."

"What? You want all of it? Are you crazy?" Darlene shouted into the phone.

"Think about it," Alice said. "It's really a pretty good offer. You'd still have the house and the stock—and you wouldn't be in jail."

There was a tense moment of silence and then Darlene said, "I'll be there in four hours."

"I'll be here waiting for you. And Darlene, come alone. I don't want to see David with you. If he's in the car when you pull up, I'm calling 911—got it?" Alice demanded.

"Yah, I got it."

"See you in four hours," Alice said and hung up.

So, we had four hours before Darlene would arrive. Say three and a half, just to be safe. I didn't trust Darlene to just come out here and write a blank check in exchange for the mask. She'd killed one person. I didn't think she'd have any hesitation in killing another one. I didn't like it, but there was no question about it—we needed a gun. Alice had never owned or even fired a gun. I however, did have one.

I drove home, got my Colt 44, and hurried back to Alice's. While I was gone, Alice had located the mace canister she'd purchased when she was first divorced. She'd never tried it, so we hoped it worked. She slipped it in her jacket pocket.

Alice had also set up her tape recorder in the living room. She kept one at the house to dictate letters. It was small and she was able to conceal it in the dried basket of flowers on the table. We figured she could turn it on when Darlene pulled into the driveway. That way we'd have everything Darlene said on tape for Cavanaugh. We'd thought about taping the phone conversation, but the recorder wasn't set up to tape over the phone. That's probably because it's illegal to surreptitiously tape a phone conversation in Illinois. That not only meant a taped phone conversation couldn't be used as evidence, it meant we could have been charged with a criminal offense if we'd made the recording. No, taping Darlene in person was the way to go.

It was four o'clock and we still hadn't heard from Cavanaugh. The receptionist must not have been able to reach him. We called his office again and this time we left a detailed message about exactly what we'd found and what we planned to do.

I hid my Jeep in the barn so Darlene would think Alice was alone. Then we selected my hiding position, behind the dense evergreens just outside the living room windows.

Our plan was to confront Darlene with the mask and get her to talk about the murder. When we had her confession on tape, I'd come in with my gun pointed at her—and we'd have Darlene. She hadn't used a gun to kill George, so we didn't think she'd bring one with her today.

Darlene hadn't asked for directions to Alice's place—she knew where she was going. I hoped we did as well.

163

We checked the sight lines from the bushes lining the windows in the other rooms, just to be sure we had the best set up. We stuck with our original choice of the living room. The count-down began. It was five-forty-five. I crouched in the semi-darkness behind the tallest juniper framing Alice's living room windows. The damp October air was already making me cold.

I could see Alice sitting at the living room table. She had a glass of wine in her hand and the black bag on the table in front of her. We'd agreed that under no circumstances should Alice leave the living room. That way she'd stay in my line of sight.

A long half hour later, I heard a car coming and signaled Alice by tapping on the window. Alice turned on the tape recorder and took her place at the table.

Car lights shined on the driveway as a black BMW pulled up to the house. Darlene and David got out. I'd hoped that wouldn't happen, but I can't say I was too surprised. I wondered if Alice had noticed. We didn't have an alternative plan, so we'd just have to proceed. I didn't see any other choice at this point.

Alice had heard the car and was going to the door before they knocked. I saw the door open onto the front porch.

"Darlene, I told you to come alone. This was supposed to be between you and me," Alice said.

"Yah, well, you don't get to make all the rules. I thought you'd of figured that out by now," Darlene said, with a nasty laugh.

I willed Alice to move closer to the table, closer to me. My prayer was answered—all three of them were now in view. Alice looked frightened—more than she should have—and then I saw why.

David had a gun drawn and was pointing it at Alice.

"So where's this mask?" Darlene said.

"Here, in the bag," Alice said, pointing to the far edge of the table in front of her.

"You know, it's too bad you found this thing—too bad for you, I mean," David said.

"So what did you do? Did you wear this to fool George?" Alice asked David.

Good girl, I thought. She was going to get them on tape.

"What are you, stupid? That mask wouldn't fool anyone up close. The mask was just so no one could recognize Darlene in the parking lot."

"So you two called George?" Alice prompted David.

"No, not me sweetheart," David said. "She did," he said pointing his gun toward Darlene.

"Darlene, you called George at the riding stable?" Alice said, looking at her.

"Yah, before he left the house I told him I had a surprise for him and to answer his phone," Darlene said. "I'd surprised him before and he liked that. I knew he'd go along with whatever I said."

"And so which one of you was in the car?" Alice asked.

They looked at each other.

"It doesn't matter," David said to Darlene. "You can tell her. Alice here is going to have a sudden attack of conscience and take a big drink of this," David said, pulling a flask from his pocket with his left hand. He kept the gun aimed at Alice. "She won't be repeating our little story to anyone after that."

"I was in the car wearing the mask," Darlene said. "George thought it was a bad joke. He told me to toss the thing, said he didn't want to see Max anymore than he had to. We drove over to the park, where George was expecting me to give him his surprise. I took off the mask and handed him a glass of gin. He took a big sip of his drink. It didn't take long and he was out. Then, I just waited for David. He took a taxi to the park and walked over to where we'd agreed I'd be waiting in the car. We drove up here with George sleeping like a baby in the front seat," Darlene said.

She continued her story saying, "The rest was easy. Drive up to the pond. Grab the poker from your kitchen. You know, you really ought to get a new hiding place for the key. Everyone knows you keep it under the mat. Anyone could let themselves in here."

"What if I'd come down?" Alice asked.

"That would have been an unfortunate murder-suicide then, wouldn't it?" David said and laughed. "Not too much different than what's going to happen right now." He moved closer to Alice and handed the flask to her.

"Open this and pour it in your glass," he said.

165

Alice glanced at the window. I knew she couldn't see out because of the reflected lights from the living room, but I hoped she felt some comfort from my presence.

I watched Alice take the flask and pour the contents into her glass.

"Now, why don't you have a good long drink?" David said.

Alice picked up the glass.

"Here's to you," she said and tossed the drink into David's face.

David screamed, "Shit," and wiped his face with his free hand.

Alice ran toward the kitchen. I fired a shot through the living room window toward the ceiling to distract David and Darlene, then I ran to the kitchen door. Alice had just reached the door. I opened it, grabbed her hand, and pulled her out of the house. I saw Darlene come into the kitchen, but she didn't run out after us. I figured she didn't have a gun.

David was flipping light switches trying to turn on the outside lights. Alice and I crouched behind the far side of Darlene's car.

Car lights came up the drive—I prayed it was Cavanaugh. As he pulled up behind Darlene's car I saw it was him. He must have finally gotten our messages. I yelled to him.

Cavanaugh stayed low as he got out of his car and crouched next to us. We quickly filled him in on the situation. A shot rang out though the living room window towards us.

"I'm going after David," Cavanaugh said. You two stay here."

"I'm going after Darlene," I said.

"You are not!" Alice said. "Leave that to Cavanaugh. He has a gun."

"So do I," I said and ran back to the house.

I braced myself against the outside wall and looked in the kitchen window. Darlene had turned off the kitchen lights. Had she left when we did? Or was she still in there?

"Darlene?" I called into the kitchen. No answer.

I opened the door and went in.

There was a swoosh and I felt a blow to my right arm. My gun went skittering to the floor. I looked in the direction of the blow and saw a ghostly figure. Darlene was barely visible in the moonlight coming through the kitchen window. She raised the fireplace shovel again for a second blow. I moved out of the way and rolled to the floor. I searched with my hands along the wooden floor in the direction I thought the gun had gone. I could hear two shots from the direction of the living room. Cavanaugh yelled to David to throw out his gun.

I had to find my gun. I moved to the side of the fireplace and put my hand on something—cat food. Too late, I'd grabbed the cold mashed meat. I wiped my hand on my jeans. Darlene was screaming again for David. Another shot rang from the living room. Cavanaugh had David's full attention. I felt the water bowl, then something—yes, my gun. It had skittered across the floor and landed along the side of the fireplace. I grabbed it and rose to my feet.

"All right Darlene, the game's over. Put the shovel down."

Darlene threw the metal fireplace shovel at me and ran out the door. I was prepared this time and side stepped the missile, then ran out the door after Darlene. I heard a grunt and a scream. Darlene was sprawled on the ground with Alice's arms around her ankles.

I stood over the two of them with my gun pointed at Darlene.

"I played football growing up," Alice said, laughing with relief.

Two more shots rang out and we heard a scream. David staggered out the living room door onto the front porch, clutching his right arm. Detective Cavanaugh was right behind him with his gun trained on the wounded man. Cavanaugh had entered the house by the side door and shot David.

I kept the gun trained on Darlene and yelled, "Detective, we're out here. We have Darlene."

Cavanaugh locked David in the back of the squad car then came over and placed handcuffs on Darlene.

Chapter 33

Happy Trails

The ambulance arrived about twenty minutes later. The same volunteer crew who'd carried away George's body now secured David on a stretcher. They lifted him into the ambulance and left quickly with their siren wailing. The ambulance was followed out the drive by the sheriff's car with its blue lights swirling. Darlene was handcuffed, sitting in the back seat, heading for jail.

"Well, I think we got it right this time," I said, as Alice, Detective Cavanaugh, and I stood watching the lights disappear down Alice's driveway.

"That tape will convince any jury if this case gets to trial. But I don't think it will. They know they can't win. They'll cut a deal with the State's Attorney," Cavanaugh said. "We'd found a few other things that didn't square with Max being our killer," he continued. "Dale told us she went to the conference lectures on Friday and sat in the back. She said she wasn't feeling well and skipped the cocktail party. We've been checking with people at the conference and we found someone who saw Dale at one of the lectures. We were following David and Darlene as well. They were seeing a lot of each other—and neither of them has a solid alibi for the time of George's murder. Darlene said she was home waiting for George. David said he was at the gym, but no one could confirm seeing him there after one o'clock."

"Well, thank God this has turned out the way it did."

"That's for sure," Alice said.

"You know what? We need a good vacation," I said.

"Some quiet time sounds great to me. Where do you want to go?" Alice said. We were getting punchy as the adrenaline began to fade.

"Kauai is beautiful. Nothing like this happens there," I said, laughing from sheer relief.

"Sounds good to me," Alice said.

"Want to join us Detective?" I asked.

"I'd like to, but I'd better get down to the station and call the State's Attorney."

We hugged our good-byes.

As the detective drove away, Alice asked, "How about a drink?"

"Good idea," I said, "but let's go over to my place to have it!"

Ordering Additional Copies of "Murder in Galena"

You may purchase autographed copies of Murder in Galena by using the form printed on this page.

MURDER IN GALENA

Mail Order Form

Please send me _____ autographed copies of Murder in Galena.

I enclose $15.50 for each copy.

Shipping Charges are $2.50 per book.
Please add 6.25% state sales tax if shipped within Illinois.

Send my book(s) to:

Name: _____

Street Address: _____

City and State: _____

Zip Code: _____

Mail this form to: Sandra Principe
P O BOX 18
GALENA, IL 61036

About The Author

Sandra Principe lives with her husband in the countryside near Galena. A Chicago lawyer for twenty years, she moved to the Galena area in 1996 to write and paint. She received her Bachelor of Science in English Education and her Juris Doctorate Degree from the University of Wisconsin, Madison.

Ms. Principe's paintings have been shown in galleries and museums across the country from Florida to California. This novel is a unique combination of her special knowledge of Galena, Chicago, law, painting and mysteries.

Read more about Sandra Principe, her art and writing, at
www.sandraprincipe.com

Printed in the United States
125728LV00002B/2/A